Lions

Bottle Boy

All it needed was one window left slightly open. Just one. Mouse had that feeling in his stomach. It was pointless hoping that the house would be securely locked. They never were. On this airless August night windows were bound to be wide open.

Suddenly a hand darted out, seizing Mouse by the scruff of his neck and hauling him across to the waste stack - the biggest external pipe and the easiest to climb.

"Up you go, monkey," Vinnie half growled, half whispered into the boy's ear. "Top floor. Bathroom window. Open as wide as Jinks's gob."

BOTTLE BOY

STEPHEN ELBOZ

Lions

An imprint of HarperCollinsPublishers

First published in Great Britain
by Oxford University Press 1994
First published in Lions 1995

1 3 5 7 9 10 8 6 4 2

Lions is an imprint of HarperCollins Children's Books,
part of HarperCollins Publishers Ltd,
77-85 Fulham Palace Road, Hammersmith,
London W6 8JB

ISBN O OO 674814-7

Printed and bound in Great Britain by
HarperCollins Manufacturing, Glasgow

To Martin Holmes
with special thanks for his help
and encouragement

CHAPTER ONE

When they told Mouse he was an orphan, he didn't know what to do or say, so he stared down at his bandaged hands, wondering if he was expected to cry.

He tried to remember something—anything—but nothing came. The truth was, he could no more remember the terrible accident at the railway crossing, than he could the two people killed in it, who were his parents. His mind had been wiped clean. It was as if he had lived his entire life in that crisp hospital bed and now had to learn everything again from new. Simple things. Like the fact he had a big brother called Vinnie, who had been pulled from the blazing car too.

To help Mouse, it was arranged by the doctors that the two brothers should meet as soon as possible. The doctors hoped the meeting would restore at least some of Mouse's memory. But Mouse merely saw a stranger, while Vinnie stared back at him in silent resentment. Later, in secret, Vinnie tattooed himself with a pin, painfully scratching two words upon his arm. MUM and DAD. At least *he* would never forget.

The accident happened nearly three years ago; now Vinnie had turned twenty-one. Mouse was twelve, although small for his age. Vinnie nicknamed him Mouse after the accident. There was a slant of viciousness in him doing so.

Together, they lived above Pinner's Old Tyme Mart. Mouse's room had a mattress on bare boards; and along a dingy corridor lay a squalid bathroom without a light.

The entire place was alive with vermin. All food had to be hidden in metal biscuit tins. In winter the pipes froze, and the cheap plywood partition walls were a fire disaster waiting to happen. It was a depressing, brooding building: a network of dark passages and unlit corners. Sometimes Mouse lay awake for hours crying for a broken past he couldn't piece together, but one which must have been so different to this.

Upstairs, apart from their rooms, stock was stored. The mice chewed through the cardboard boxes. Downstairs was what the public saw. *Herod Pinner's Old Tyme Mart.*

Once it had been an old Victorian boot factory, although now the brick walls were painted white, with fake half-timbering tacked on, both inside and out. The shelves were stacked with clocks, coronation mugs, teapots, and prints torn from old books, along with larger pieces of furniture. Everything was set out in order, making it resemble what in fact it actually was: a supermarket for antiques. Not even real antiques in most cases but reproductions, machine-made in Eastern sweat-shops. Designed to look Englishy and hand-crafted. Fakes three times over.

Mouse was required to earn his keep. ('Can't carry no dead weight,' said Pinner.) He filled shelves, unpacked boxes, swept, and was generally the one who fetched and carried. Occasionally he was trusted to do a more demanding chore like *distressing*—the name given to the act of vandalizing a perfectly good piece of furniture in order to make it look old and, of course, more expensive. Like the regular Saturday boys he was obliged to dress in a costume that made him resemble a character out of *Oliver Twist*; and the bored girls on the tills were milkmaids in aprons and mob caps.

Everything was fake at Pinner's—including the staff.

And Mouse, who knew nothing different

and could not remember anything better, worked all day here. It was his life. He spoke to few people. He had no friends. He thought it would be like this . . . always . . .

It was a Tuesday when the old man appeared, panting and blundering into things with his carrier bags. Clearly he was in to browse. Mouse knew this by the way he mulled over the odd few genuinely old items, his thick callous hands familiar with the feel of them.

Slowly he moved down the aisles, then stopped to gaze in amazement at a display of empty beer bottles.

'The world's gone mad,' he announced in a wheezy voice to no one in particular but, since Mouse stood nearby, he glanced up and shyly smiled back at him.

The old man took this for encouragement.

'Utterly mad,' he went on. Picking up one of the old bottles, he felt the embossed name and trade mark of the long-extinct brewery like a blind man reading braille. 'I wurn't much older than you when I 'ad m'first strong drink,' he recalled. 'It wur from a bottle sim'lar to this 'un. That makes y'think, don' it?—We're as ancient as each other. But see 'ow much they're askin' for these now. Empty bottles which once we threw away without a second thought.'

He sighed. Mouse nodded sympathetically.

Quite unexpectedly the old man winked at him and shuffled a few steps nearer.

'You're a bright-looking lad,' he said. 'I'll tell you summat worth your while—not a story, mind, but summat for real. 'Istory now, I suppose.' And mysteriously lowering his voice, he went on: 'When I wur a lad all them years ago, I lived near this big place called Coldby Hall. And me ol' dad before me, 'e worked in the gardens there. Any'ow, even before 'is time there wur this lake behind the hall where the son o' the 'ouse used to swim. He 'ad this fondness for swimming at night, see? And one night he swims to the middle o' the lake and 'e must 'ave got cramp.'

'He drowned?' said Mouse, suddenly curious.

The old man nodded. ''Is father were that 'eartbroken 'e orders the lake be drained and filled in. And when land-owning folk gave orders in them days it wur like a law to be carried out. So they drained away the water and over some time the hole wur filled in using rubbish from the nearby towns and villages—well, it wur rubbish in them days. Filled it right t'the brim they did. I tell you, there must be plenty o' bottles like these lying in the ground. Waiting like buried treasure. If I wur younger—a young enterprising lad like yourself—I'd get me a good spade and go there. I'd dig me out some. There ken't be no easier way o' making an honest bob or two. That's a fact.'

He chuckled to himself.

As he reached up to replace the bottle his hand began to tremble.

'Watch it!' cried Mouse.

Before the boy could help him, the bottle slipped from the old man's grasp, knocking down another as it fell. They struck the floor and shattered, the sound audible across the entire shop. Horrified, Mouse dropped to his knees and started collecting the broken pieces of glass with his bare hands.

'Here, let me help you, son,' muttered the old man, trying to bend his knees and get down alongside him.

'No . . . no. It's fine. It's okay,' said Mouse distractedly. 'Just go. Please. I'll manage.'

He kept glancing up, wishing desperately for the old man to leave him. It would only be a matter of time before Pinner bore down upon the scene with his nasty professional smile and hard all-seeing eyes. But the old man hovered there fretting and apologizing.

'Somethin' up?' growled a voice. *Pinner*. He had crept up and was standing there watching: a great bear of a man in a loose baggy suit with lots of ugly jewellery. He rested his elbow on a shelf. At midday he already looked in need of a second shave.

'S-sorry, Mr P-Pinner,' stammered Mouse. 'An accident. I'll clean it up i-immediately.'

'See that you do,' grunted Pinner—the warning tone barely disguised. 'Then step along to m'office.'

With these words he turned and strode off.

Mouse was not the heroic type, far from it, so he wondered why he had taken the blame. Then, glancing across at the old man, all red and flustered, wringing his mottled hands, he knew it was because Pinner would have expected him to pay for the breakages. A large sign by the door demanded it. Perhaps Mouse took the blame on himself in return for the moment's interest. Perhaps for the tale.

'Don't get yourself into no trouble on my account, son,' fretted the old man. 'Don't get yourself sacked.'

'I won't be sacked,' said Mouse glumly.

Five minutes later he stood timidly knocking outside Pinner's door. His knees felt weak. Pinner had lashed out at him before now. His rings had left marks on his skin.

'In!'

Mouse meekly entered the ultra-modern office. It was cold and chromed and starkly white, like a laboratory; for Pinner's sights were firmly set on the future and he detested old-fashioned things nearly as much as he despised the customers who bought them. Mouse's heart sank further when he saw Vinnie slumped in a leather chair, one of his long legs swinging loosely over its arm. He didn't turn to look at Mouse but stared out of the big plate glass window. Pinner was behind his desk signing something, deliberately taking his time before clicking the top on his pen and tucking it away into an inside pocket.

'Ah,' he said, looking up over folded hands. 'If it ain't the boy with the butter fingers. The butter-fingered boy. You know what 'appens to unpaid breakages, boy? Eh? Well, I'll tell ya. They eats into m'profits and I go 'ungry. Boys with butter fingers should take proper care.'

'S-sorry, Mr Pinner, I won't let—'

'You can't bank no sorries, boy,' he growled. 'You owe me one—you owe me one in return. Ain't in the charity game. Not 'ere.'

Mouse felt a horrible churning inside him. He knew what was coming.

'P-please, Mr Pinner—'

'He'll do it,' snapped Vinnie absently. He went on gazing out of the window, swinging his leg. It was as if Mouse wasn't in the same room.

'Tonight,' said Pinner. He took out his pen again and continued to write. 'And you best make sure you ain't so clumsy this time.'

'No . . . Mr Pinner,' mumbled Mouse obediently. He hovered, waiting to be dismissed.

'Get lost, Mouse,' said Vinnie.

Mouse backed away without a sound.

CHAPTER TWO

Oh yes, one of Mr Pinner's *special* jobs. Not the usual line for a shelf-filling drudge. Yet it was the main reason big brother Vinnie kept Mouse tagging along. Mouse, you see, was an experienced burglar. It was his slightness of build that made him so good—that gave him access to places too small for a grown man. Once inside, Mouse knew how to turn off burglar alarms; then it was simply a case of unlocking a door and letting Vinnie in. Vinnie, working all the time for Pinner, lifted only what was wanted: some Dresden china, perhaps, or a pair of George III candlesticks; occasionally something bigger like a piece of furniture. Something for which there was a specific need—and before morning it would be packed up, ready for sending to some foreign client, who neither knew nor cared how it had been obtained.

What it was to be that particular night,

Mouse had no idea. He never knew. That side of the business wasn't his concern; he was merely the one who opened the door. To keep a clear head for later, Vinnie insisted that he got some rest. Mouse slept uneasily until a foot nudged him awake. He lay on his mattress looking up at the dark, menacing figure standing over him.

'Get up,' said Vinnie.

Mouse pulled on his jeans and followed Vinnie down the dark, rickety staircase. He stayed close. Vinnie lit the way with a flashlight.

Outside, highly polished chrome gleamed in the yard. Two motor bikes rested heavily on their stands. The second machine belonged to Jinks, the third member of the gang. Jinks, although the same age as Vinnie, was stooped and crooked, his grin a permanent fixture, even when he lost his rag. Seeing Mouse, he looked up from adjusting some oily component on his bike and his grin widened for a moment.

Mouse ignored him. He was the one person the boy was allowed to treat with contempt.

Jinks said in his mumbling way, 'What's it to be tonight, Vin?'

'Snuff boxes,' replied Vinnie, stuffing the address Pinner had given him into a pocket and zipping it up.

Jinks's jaw dropped, making him look even more stupid. 'Snuff boxes? Wass snuff when it's at 'ome?'

'Snuff's what they used in the old days,' said Mouse without thinking. 'It's like your roll-ups, Jinks. 'Cept you sniff the tobacco stuff up your nose. You'd be good at that, Jinks. You're always sniffing.'

'Liar!' cried Jinks, grinning in disbelief.

And Vinnie said darkly, 'Don't need no history lessons.'

In silence Mouse put on Vinnie's spare crash helmet, strapping it beneath his chin. He slipped behind Vinnie on the saddle. Both bikes suddenly roared into life, their riders revving hard; then with a jolt Mouse found himself propelled from the yard into the empty street. Vinnie's machine sliced the night. Street lights flashed rhythmically overhead. Jinks, riding alongside, grinned slyly.

Out of town, Vinnie loosened the throttle as they raced each other across the countryside. In waves, Mouse smelt hay or the melted tar of the road. He curled his fingers under the pillion, solid air slamming into his face whenever he looked up.

Twenty minutes later they reached Hingham, an over-grown market town straddling a wide main street, with the modern estates tucked away out of sight. The two headlights died as the bikes glided to a halt in the shadows.

Beneath a street light Vinnie took out the scrap of paper to study it again. He also had a photograph of the desired snuff boxes. Then they set off, briskly, almost running. Jinks—bow-legged, hands rattling keys in his pockets—giving a deep nod at every step; and Mouse, seemingly forgotten, scurrying along behind. Yet whenever a car went by he was sure to be manhandled into the nearest doorway. Once a police-car prowled the distant kerbside and Mouse felt Vinnie's grip tighten around his arm until it hurt.

Finally they stopped before a stone cottage.

'This it?' grinned Jinks.

Vinnie nodded absently. He stood staring at a wall on the garden side then, without a word, went forward and hoisted himself over it.

'It's okay,' they heard him whisper from the other side.

Jinks gave a nervous snigger before following. Then hands reached back to seize Mouse, roughly dragging him into a dark courtyard.

Instinctively the three stood close together. Mouse saw that high walls formed all but one of the courtyard's sides. Against them spindly roses clung and further back stood the dark hump of a caravan. The courtyard's fourth side was created by the cottage itself. All windows curtained and dark.

Jinks and Mouse remained still, hardly daring to move, but Vinnie slid across to the base of the house. Mouse was unable to see him but knew well enough what he was doing. He was planning the route for him to take. All it needed was one window left slightly open. Just one. Mouse had *that* feeling in his stomach. It was pointless hoping that the house would be securely locked. They never were. On this airless August night windows were bound to be wide open.

Suddenly a hand darted out, seizing Mouse by the scruff of his neck and hauling him across to the waste stack—the biggest external pipe and the easiest to climb.

'Up you go, monkey,' Vinnie half growled, half whispered into the boy's ear. 'Top floor. Bathroom window. Open as wide as Jinks's gob.'

'Ge-urr,' sneered Jinks.

Before releasing him, Vinnie gave Mouse his usual parting promise: 'Wake ony'un up and you're on y'own. Got it?'

Mouse nodded.

Vinnie bundled him as far up the pipe as he could. Then Mouse found his grip and began to climb with ease. Soundlessly he passed the first-storey windows. He wasn't even breathless when he paused for a moment, resting a foot on a side pipe. Looking out he had a clear view over the wall to the road, which slithered silver-grey between street lamps. Below, in a pit of darkness, he could make out two up-turned faces watching his every movement.

'C'm on. Get on wi' it,' rasped a hostile voice.

But Mouse didn't move. He stood deep in thought until, almost imperceptibly, he nodded to himself.

'Wass up wi' 'im?' muttered Jinks.

Neither he nor Vinnie had any way of knowing about Mouse's decision. It had even taken the boy by surprise and, afterwards, it seemed as if a light had flashed inside his head. He was going to run away. Be free. It both alarmed and excited him to think he could take his own future into his hands—at a stroke casting off Pinner, Vinnie, and the dreary life of a fetch-and-carry boy. Not to mention the uncertain career of a thief. It was all to do with that old man—or rather his story and the half hope it might be true. First things first, however: he must make good his escape.

He began to climb again; this time there

was something joyful about his movements.

'Mouse!' called a harsh voice as he shinned past the opened window. 'What you playing at? Eh?' Vinnie sounded more puzzled than annoyed.

Mouse started edging along the stone course where the roof overhung the wall. He reached up, curling his fingers around the guttering. Hesitating a moment he took the risk, swinging out his legs—kicking against the stonework. As soon as he did, he felt the guttering give and slightly move away from the eaves.

Unthinkingly—without time to be afraid— his right foot came up, lodging by the heel in the guttering itself. The guttering shuddered again, more violently this time, and Mouse felt the cast iron disintegrate beneath him, sending gritty flakes of rust into the eyes of Vinnie and Jinks, who cursed.

With hands splayed, the boy blindly fumbled amongst the roof tiles for something higher and firmer to grip. The guttering creaked. He had seconds to find it.

Jamming his fingers into a broken tile, he pulled up with all his might, trusting to the strength of his hands. He pulled until his arms shook and the muscles in his stomach ached. Sweat broke out on his face. Yet no longer was he dangling in the air but spread flat upon the roof's gentle slope, his final kick accidentally wrenching the guttering away from the wall. He heard it crash on the paving slabs below.

Lying there, his cheek against the mossy tiles, he wondered if it had struck Vinnie. The thought made him smile. It had certainly stirred them up. Cowards. Jinks and his brother were running away. Saving their own skins. Each one knocking the other aside as they scrambled over the wall. Then their boots were heard echoing down the deserted street.

However, Mouse had no time to congratulate himself. A door was hurriedly unbolted and someone stepped out into the courtyard to investigate the noise.

'What was it, George?' called a woman from an upper window. She sounded worried.

'The old guttering's down,' reported her husband glumly, his slippers crunching on flakes of rotting iron. 'A pound to a penny it was a cat.'

'A cat? Why on earth should a cat be on our roof?'

'Have sense, woman,' answered the man curtly. 'Cats have territories, don't they? Well, at least this one's kissed goodbye to several of its nine lives.'

'Me-ow!'

Despite the danger, Mouse couldn't resist

it. Just the once. Then he covered his mouth with his hand.

'See . . . see!' cried the man excitedly. 'A damn moggie. What did I tell you? We ought to put pepper down.'

'On the roof?' said his wife incredulously.

A few more grumbles later and the man had gathered up the broken pieces of ironwork and returned to bed, depressed at the thought of replacing it. Then the bedroom light went out.

Mouse had no watch but guessed he lay there for another fifteen minutes. Eventually, when certain no one was awake to hear him, he crawled on all fours to the chimney, and by the shadowy roadside light surveyed his kingdom.

He discovered himself at the end of a terrace, the roofs of the other buildings forming a broken line before him. The first three roofs were more or less on the same level. The fourth roof dropped a good storey lower.

Stealthily he moved along the ridge to the roof of the adjoining building. This was of thin Welsh slate and creaked like ice at every move, so that the boy half expected to plunge through it at any moment. He was relieved to reach the thatched top of the third building. It didn't matter that it pricked and scratched: he felt as safe as if astride a great haystack.

On its street side he noticed two rounded hummocks that, like baskets, wove themselves around two dormer windows. Leaning back and using the roof's natural slope in his favour, Mouse eased himself down to the nearest of these. The window was open far enough for his hand to squeeze through. He reached in and opened it wide. Slipping inside he found himself in a bedroom—the toys on the shelves revealing it to be the bedroom of a young child—and to his horror Mouse saw a small figure sitting up in bed, watching him. Sleep blurred his expression, making him look oddly fierce.

'Who are you?' demanded the child in a loud ringing voice that made Mouse wince, almost to the point of rushing across to plead for silence. Instead he surprised himself by whispering back, 'Shh! I'm a dream.'

'Am I dreaming you?' asked the child, lowering his voice to a puzzled whisper.

'Yeah. That's it. In the morning I won't be here and you'll 'ave forgotten me.'

'Oh,' said the child in a sleepy, reassured way and laying down his head drifted straight off to sleep again.

Mouse watched over him for a few moments. When certain he wouldn't stir, he slipped through the door, felt his way down the staircase and found the kitchen. For the first time he switched on a light. As the strip light flickered he panicked slightly—as if he had surprised himself doing something he ought not. Quickly he stuffed a carrier-bag with food along with some other things that might come in useful. A knife, a tin opener, a box of matches and the loose change from the window-sill.

The front door clicked as he stepped out on to the street. He gulped down a deep breath of air to calm himself. So the adventure is under way, he thought. Already Vinnie and Jinks were as distant as memories—Pinner a bad dream.

Removing an unused bin-liner from a dustbin, he tucked it away inside his jacket and walked on until the town was behind him. He found a country church standing away from a cluster of cottages. He wasn't at all afraid of the broken, flaking gravestones. Indeed, after slipping into the dustbin liner, he snuggled up to the tomb of one Jacob Cornhill who, according to the inscription, lived an exemplary life and died in 1834.

Mouse, however, had no mind to dwell on past lives. He was thinking ahead to the future. And treasure. If old beer bottles made a poor sort of treasure, it was treasure none the less.

CHAPTER THREE

Mouse awoke confused and startled. Raucous cries like the barking of dogs filled his ears and above his opening eyes something dark and broken came descending. He struggled to sit up, crumbs of soil clinging to his hair.

Crows surrounded him, bad-natured and black; skulking through the overgrown grass between headstones, squawking and snapping at each other, full of spite and jealousy.

Blinking the sleep away, Mouse saw that they had ripped into his bag of supplies. Pieces of sliced bread littered the grass and still they returned to the bag to pull out something new.

'Hey! That's my food!' he cried.

As a brood, the crows turned their eyes on him. Knowing their windfall to be ended they began gobbling hard, each one trying to snatch a last beak-full as Mouse chased them away.

Angrily, Mouse grabbed up an apple, its

flesh already browning where the crows had pecked through the skin, and hurled it as hard as he could at the nearest scavenging bird. It missed by miles, splattering against the church wall, his anger exploding with it. Calmly he stood thinking of what he should do. He must find that old house. Coldby Hall. He must know for sure whether it really existed, or was just an old man's romancing.

At the next village he stopped an old grandad on a bicycle, a bored young mother with a push-chair, and a woman waiting for a bus. None had heard of Coldby Hall. The woman with the push-chair misunderstood completely and thought Coldby Hall was an American soap star.

'Try the library, son,' called the old man, unsteadily setting off again on his clanking prehistoric bicycle.

Mouse frowned. Best, he thought, to avoid such places. In the past Vinnie had taught him to distrust authority, if only the authority of a librarian to insist on silence. Besides, there was always the risk of meeting Pinner or his brother in town. He certainly didn't want to chance that.

Yet for all his reserve, Mouse had learnt to be resourceful—even cunning whenever the occasion arose. He found a phone-box—one of those country phone-boxes existing in the middle of nowhere. Dialling the operator, he carefully explained that he had just put money into the machine and it wouldn't allow his call or return his coin. The operator sounded dubious but, in the end, agreed to connect him.

'Just the one call, mind,' she said briskly.

'Only need one,' replied Mouse, managing to sound indignant that she should question his honesty.

He phoned a taxi firm whose card had been slipped beneath the glass of the shelf.

A woman answered.

'I want to go to Coldby Hall,' he announced (failing to mention that he wouldn't need a taxi to do so). 'Er, can you tell me, is it far?'

The woman told him she hadn't heard of Coldby Hall, but if he meant the village of Coldby it was about fourteen miles away. With a little more prompting, she even gave Mouse directions and told him which roads to take.

'Ta,' said Mouse, quickly putting the receiver down.

By now it was noon. Dense hazy heat pressed on the boy, weighing him down as if it were a burden to be carried. He ran a finger along his collar, the mere thought of all those miles wearying him as he considered the endless dull chore of placing one foot in front of the other. His mouth was dry and he remembered that he hadn't drunk since the previous day. Later, when he heard water, he fell down on his knees, lapping at the cold spring like an animal. Then he allowed himself three biscuits from his precious store and resumed his journey, walking towards the featureless distance.

Presently he reached a main road. There his plodding progress was in marked contrast to the steady flow of traffic; and the bigger lorries, as they raced by, caused such a rush of air that he was almost sucked off his feet. The people in the cars stared at him as if at a curiosity—which he was: the bedraggled boy with the torn carrier-bag, squinting his eyes at the dust, tripping on the uneven verges; and once a discarded apple core struck him on the back of his head.

However, this indignity was quickly forgotten when next he lifted his eyes. For the first time he saw the name Coldby. It was on a roadsign and the sun, now behind him, caused the sign to reflect its light. The name itself seemed to be shining.

His hopes rekindled and feeling stupidly happy (perhaps hunger was making him light-headed), he turned off on to a twisting country lane, expecting at every bend to see Coldby loom up before him.

But Coldby was not as easily reached as that. It was nearly dark when finally he arrived there. His initial feeling was disappointment. All his efforts for such little reward. Somehow he felt cheated. Why, Coldby wasn't even a proper village—more a hamlet, without a shop, pub, or church. Mouse simply couldn't accept the handful of brick and stone cottages straggling a deserted green, even though they must have housed the old workers of the Coldby estate (for each one bore the same coat of arms and large swirling monogram). The question now was, where would he find the hall?

Passing through the hamlet, Mouse continued a little further along the road until it brought him to a gate-house. It was like a small castle dropped by the roadside. Grey and empty, it was nearly a ruin and its gates were rusted and chained. Mouse smiled. He didn't need gates to open for him. He could climb like a cat.

He jumped down.

On the far side, the carriage track was little more than a crease in the grass, overhung by low, sweeping trees.

'No goin' back,' Mouse told himself, if only to be reassured by the sound of his own voice. The trees moved overhead and shut out the sky.

Beyond the trees came a long slow climb to a breezy ridge, the highest point in the district. Standing there, Mouse had a clear view of what he searched for: a large greystone building set in the hollow where four hills met. Its windows were tall and regular and a balustrade of lighter-coloured stone crowned its upper parts. From a high double door swept a mossy flight of steps, disappearing into unkempt rose gardens; while a vegetable plot, as incongruous as a suburban allotment, was set right against the wall of the house itself. Weeds thronged the gravel paths and from their stone urns geraniums glowed deep blood red. For all its many rooms, only one light was lit—a flickering oil lamp at a downstairs window.

Mouse studied the house carefully, wondering in which direction the old lake might lie. By the look of it, the hall had extensive grounds and it might prove difficult to find. From his high vantage point he then noticed a dark swathe of trees forming a semi-circle beyond the old house. This would solve a more immediate problem: shelter for the night. Pushing aside his worries he made tracks towards it. Night was descending rapidly now, and soon he lost sight of his destination, even as he came nearer to it.

Then all at once the trees took shape,

ancient broad-leaved trees standing as if becalmed. Mouse, stumbling along a half-hidden track, found a tangle of barbed wire blocking his way. From the wire rose a sign. The paint was peeling but its message clear: *Jerusalem Wood. Private. Keep Out.* Mouse felt it didn't apply to him, only the rest of the world.

Skirting the wood, he eventually discovered a gap big enough to squeeze through. Then he had to chart his own route through dense undergrowth. Until he knew better he tripped on roots and blundered into low branches. It was as if he was trying to master a new way of walking—like sea legs. But he liked the closeness of the trees. He liked the rich, musty smell his feet kicked up from the leaf mould. And best of all he liked the promise of secrecy offered by the powerful silence . . .

Suddenly his happiness was dashed. Ahead he saw lights.

It was in a part of the wood that sloped down. The trees were tall and spindly. He saw lights and at the same time heard voices. His first thoughts were to turn around and go, but curiosity held him, then drew him bit by bit to the edge of a clearing, where he was able to look out unobserved.

At first he couldn't understand what he was seeing. It was as if it was snowing in the middle of summer. For a moment, Mouse thought it *was* snow, but of course it wasn't. It was thistledown, released from great patches of the plant growing wild about the clearing. It formed into drifts and seemed to swell in size as it floated into the glowing light of the many lamps that were set upon the ground or hung up in the trees. Thistledown also caught in the hair and clung to the clothes of the three children who went dashing between lamps hunting the moths that were drawn instinctively to them.

Listening to their talk, Mouse soon discovered a little about them. They were sister and brothers. The oldest of the three was called Ralph. He must have been about fourteen. He wasn't so tall, but he was broad and solid with a lick of very black hair poised above a round face. He reminded Mouse of a miniature farmer for, despite the warm night, he wore a tweed jacket, waistcoat and cord trousers. Annie was the girl. She was probably Mouse's age, pale and unsmiling, and in the habit of brushing aside her hair, even when it wasn't in the way. The second boy, Clyde, was much younger: he couldn't have been more than eight years old and was fair like his sister.

Annie's hair was very long. Thistledown clung to it. She carelessly hooked it behind her ears and held up a jam jar, counting the moths that fluttered inside.

'I've got twelve!' she announced at last. 'And I'm certain one of my moths is a death's head.'

'I bet,' returned Ralph at once. 'Tell you what, old thing, I'll give you a fiver if it is—no, make it a tenner.'

Seeing himself outdone by his older brother and sister, Clyde called, 'Anyway, you two, I've caught a purple emperor.'

Ralph and Annie burst out laughing.

'What's so funny?' he demanded.

'The purple emperor is a butterfly, you dodo,' Annie shouted back.

Then, like wild children, they went scrambling between lamps, all the time shouting out to each other and laughing. Indeed they laughed a great deal.

Mouse watched and listened with envy. He was a loner by nature—an outsider. He accepted this. So why did he now feel so unsettled and dissatisfied with his lot? Deciding he had seen enough, he silently backed away and found a part of the wood where the only sound was the breeze in the branches.

There he wrapped himself in the black plastic bag and tried to sleep.

CHAPTER FOUR

Mouse's sleep ended with a sharp shiver. He awoke to discover his hair and eye-lashes beaded with dew and his clothes pressing damply against his skin. He had never experienced such cold, even during the winter in his unheated room, and the uncontrollable way his teeth rattled frightened him. Kicking free of the ineffectual black plastic, he lumbered up on to his feet, stamping the numbness from his legs and hugging his body for the little warmth there was to be had.

Eventually he grew still, his steaming breath coming in irregular gasps.

Sniffing back a drip from the end of his nose, he cast the wood a long, respectful sideways glance. He saw that he had been lying submerged beneath a dense veil of creeping mist. It was not long after dawn. Velvety-grey. And here and there softer shafts of light pierced the dense foliage.

More than food, he realized, his most

pressing need was a shelter of some kind and, as instinctively as any animal, he began the task of building one there and then. All he had to help him, beyond his own hands and wits, was a small kitchen knife; and in due course he began *if onlying*. If only he had an axe . . . some nails . . . string . . . a saw. Yet as the morning advanced he found he was enjoying the challenge of trying to resolve each problem as it arose. Once he even caught himself whistling.

He was reminded of the time before Vinnie had teamed up with Pinner and they had spent six months roughing it around the country with Jinks. One night a heavy downpour washed out their tents, so Vinnie set to, making a structure of his own from branches and turf and any oddments he happened to find or steal. Vinnie really took the task upon himself, ordering Jinks and Mouse about like a site foreman. The result was a shelter so warm and weatherproof that they were able to hole up in it for two weeks before moving on.

As Mouse struggled to create something comparable, he recalled the acrid reek of wood smoke and the mystery of a dark windowless interior. It was how prehistoric man must have lived.

With hands stained green and black from

the damp wood, he patiently wove lesser, more pliant twigs between the larger supporting branches, some of which were the living parts of a beech tree, whose trunk anchored the entire structure like a great pillar.

Gradually his hut took shape. Its lines weren't as crisp as Vinnie's, but Mouse couldn't help feeling a certain pride. It was entered by the lowest of doorways, which lay concealed from view. Inside he studied the places where light broke in and patched and mended continuously. He was like a human spider who couldn't be content with what might be improved.

Arising with the shelter came the powerful desire to protect it. Squatting before his doorway, Mouse took the long, straight branch he had specially selected and began to whittle one end into a point. Perhaps if the blade hadn't become so blunt it wouldn't have slipped along the sappy wood. But it all happened so quickly. Mouse felt a sudden sharp pain in the back of his hand. Then the brilliance of blood as it welled up. He stared at it with a mixture of horror, mortification, and intrigue.

Within seconds the pain subsided to a dull ache. Mouse found his feet as blood dripped steadily on to the dark earth. He felt dizzy enough to faint. He fought back panic. This was another fear he hadn't considered, along with the fear of hunger and cold—what if he became ill or hurt? *Get the cut washed. Get the dirt out.* He could think of nothing else as he blundered to the nearby stream. There, falling to his knees, he plunged in his arm. The cold shocked him back to his senses. Lifting his head he saw something on the other bank.

It gleamed.

It was an old bottle.

A brief search revealed two more bottles, half embedded in the mud. Mouse let his fingers feel under the dense greenery for the smooth touch of glass. Afterwards, his gashed hand forgotten, he washed his finds in the stream.

Thinking the matter over, Mouse considered the possibility that once the stream might have fed the old lake. It was certainly worth investigating. Clutching the bottles to his chest, he followed the flow of the stream between two deep banks. It was by now early afternoon and through breaks in the trees hot, bright light splashed. Mouse squinted up his eyes at it. Already he was more accustomed to the gloom.

He struggled a while to thrash a path along the stream's side, before finally giving up on it. He was much too impatient and the nettles there were quite vicious. Rolling up his jeans (yet keeping on his trainers and socks) he slipped into the stream and slowly waded out into the middle. The water was cold enough to make him gasp, while his feet sank into oozy mud, making each step a test of strength and balance.

He had no idea of what he would find. Possibly he was wrong altogether, and the bottles a lucky chance discovery. All he did know was, when he came to it, he'd somehow realize that this was the place.

And he was right.

After twenty frustrating minutes the trees abruptly ended and the stream trickled around the edge of a large clearing. Mouse clambered up the bank into the sun, warming his cold legs, the mud tightening to his skin as it dried. Shading his eyes, Mouse smiled as he took in the scene.

There was something quite eerie about it. More than the obvious silence and stillness. It was the shape of the land itself. It rose and fell in an endless series of irregular humps and troughs. Like a moonscape.

Mouse tested the ground with his heel.

''Ard as iron,' he muttered bitterly. He felt stupid. Did he really expect to see the bottles lying there? He supposed he did. Now he knew he would need to dig down to find what he was looking for. All treasure worth its while had to be dug for.

Later, trying to trace a path back to his hut, Mouse saw something that so shocked him he fell to the ground as if physically struck.

It was above him, in the trees—dark and sinister—cruelly hung up like butchers' meat on a hook. When the breeze caught it, its limbs stiffly danced, bumping into the tree trunk.

Mouse lay still as if hiding from it, trying to summon the necessary courage to look again. When he did, he realized all was not what it first appeared. Hurrying up to the figure he angrily tugged at its leg. It fell in a crumpled heap at his feet: a crudely made scarecrow, the rope still knotted around its neck, the face a grotesque mask. To it was pinned a message and Mouse had no doubt who it was intended for.

It read: 'To the Trespasser. Get out of our wood. Now!' and was signed 'The Three Pendreds'.

Mouse was blazing mad. Mad that they should consider it *their* wood to do with as they pleased, and mad that they thought him so easily scared off.

Tearing the message to shreds he shouted, 'I know who you are! I know you!'

Then he paused, his eyes blinking nervously.

More practically, however, he stripped the old raincoat from the scarecrow's stick bones, and carried it back to his hut pretending it was a spoil of war. Well, at least of the phoney war. He would have to watch how matters developed.

CHAPTER FIVE

That night, like a proud African chieftain, Mouse squatted before his hut. He had his own fire and the scarecrow's coat was carelessly draped across his shoulders like a ceremonial robe.

He examined his supplies. They were precisely this: one tin of sardines (he hated sardines), one tin of peaches, one small tin of meat balls and three potatoes (two, if he allowed for the one currently baking in the fire). No matter how he rearranged them, they never appeared more than they actually were.

When Vinnie built his hut, he and Jinks would go out at nights snaring rabbits. Mouse always begged him not to, but Vinnie told him he was soft. Perhaps he was. He'd lie awake for hours waiting for the thin, high-pitched scream as the wire caught and bit. It was an unbearable sound—almost human in its terror. One night Mouse crept out from the hut to release an ensnared creature. It was a trembling bundle of wet fur. Vinnie was furious when he found out; and next time he skinned a rabbit he flung the pelt at Mouse, catching him full in the face. With blood smearing his face and hands, Mouse worked himself into a hysterical state. Even Vinnie took fright a little, the blood reminding him of the road accident. Pinning his brother roughly to the ground, he waited until the wildness broke into a series of gulping sobs.

Mouse shook his head to clear his mind of the memory. He threw more sticks to the fire: at least that was easily fed. Thinking about food made him feel ravenously hungry. He prodded the lone black spud at the fire's edge as if bullying it into cooking faster. When he eventually ate it, it was hard in the middle and his teeth crunched on unpleasant gritty bits of ash.

His jaws moving rhythmically back and forth, Mouse fell to thinking. He remembered the old hall and its vegetable garden. He had hoped his thieving days behind him but, as he told himself in a sad, accepting way, this was a matter of survival.

Mouse waited until the moon rose before setting off. Overwhelmed by the old coat, he looked like an apprentice tramp; and as he went through the dense undergrowth he raised his arms as if breasting a fast, deep river. By the time he reached open parkland, mist was rising in the hollows. Below, a single light shone up from the hall. Like a star, Mouse used it to navigate by.

The evening stillness unleashed the scent of roses, meeting him as he crept down the hill. Then came lavender and stocks and, further on, the enticing aroma of mint and rosemary. The vegetable plot was the only part that showed it had been regularly tended. Most of the formal gardens were reverting to the wild, their statues imprisoned in briars; while the walls of the terraces crumbled into elders that burst from the mortar itself. Close to, Mouse noticed that the fabric of the old hall appeared shabby and decayed.

Led by his nose, Mouse began to gather what he could. And what did not go straight into his mouth filled the coat, which made a convenient bundle over his shoulder. Raspberries, gooseberries, peas, sticks of rhubarb, gritty radishes, and carrots; and potatoes coming out of the soil like big brown pebbles yielding themselves up.

If he needed to uproot a plant, he carefully lifted it from the end of a row, hiding the inedible parts in a reeking compost heap. Only his footprints gave him away, but he took as much care as possible.

Then, beyond a long rambling greenhouse, Mouse noticed a shack. He hoped for a tool shed where he would find a spade. But when he got there he discovered it was a chicken coop. A spade would have been useful but he was not unduly disappointed as he thought of warm, newly laid eggs. Inside, the roosting birds were silent, giving Mouse the necessary courage he needed. Slowly his hand reached out for the door, but as soon as he turned the handle chains rattled, barring his way. It was the smallest of sounds, yet its effect was remarkable. Frenzied and indignant, the chickens flew up in every direction, making such a terrible commotion that Mouse shrank back from it in horror, his hands pressed to his ears.

He never heard the scrape of a window lifting open in the big house, but suddenly a stripe of pale yellow light fell across the gardens.

'Who iz da?' demanded a thickly accented voice. 'A fox? You damn fox back again?' The voice began to mumble. 'Thiz time I fix you pretty damn good.'

Hearing the voice Mouse froze, standing transfixed to the spot. But when he glimpsed the snout of a long grey barrel thrusting out of the window towards him, he turned and fled, dropping everything he had gathered. At the same moment the gun discharged with a searing white flash and a noise that rolled over him like a powerful wave, radiating out across the darkness to the hills.

'Ach—missed!' grunted the voice disappointedly.

Mouse had been taught a lesson known already by local predators. Afterwards, the more he thought about it the more heroic the episode seemed. Convinced he had looked death in the face, Mouse laughed at his own recklessness, but on hearing an engine and seeing two headlights sweep a distant field, he automatically dropped to the ground, wondering if it was the same gun-toting madman. Slowly he realized it couldn't be. The vehicle was not coming from the direction of the hall; and when he saw its destination was Jerusalem Wood, he felt curious and suspicious. Outside the wood, the world was entitled to take pot-shots at him; after all he was no better than an unwanted stray. But the wood was different. He considered that his own territory.

At full sprint he gave chase, but never too certain of the ground, he stumbled in the darkness, each time cursing his misfootings. Luckily the vehicle—it was a Land Rover—travelled slowly too, rocking and bouncing across trackless pasture. In its headlights cows loomed as large as boulders. Only as they rose in their elegant disgruntled way to escape the intruding glare, did they become recognizable farm animals once more.

Soon the headlights flickered behind tall, black, angular trees. Coming across a patch of soft earth, Mouse saw tyre prints, many prints, criss-crossing each other, but all belonging to the same vehicle. They pointed towards a track leading into the wood. Pausing a moment to regain his breath, Mouse went down it close on the Land Rover's red, glowing tail lights. In a sinister way they resembled devilish eyes glaring back at him.

And so he arrived, shortly after the Land Rover itself, at the wide clearing where the lake had been. By night the hummocky ground appeared more strikingly like a place on the moon than before; and the horizontal headlight beams slashing across the darkness added a tantalizing mystery. Who was it and why were they here?

At once doors opened and voices spilled out. Mouse crouched on the ground to watch. *The enemy!* It was *the enemy*. The three Pendred kids. Ralph first, followed by Annie. Nervously she stroked her elbows, her fringe in her eyes. Last of all came Clyde, carelessly swinging round his legs to sit on the door sill, and clearly not happy.

'Why do we have to come here so late, Ralph?' he wailed.

'I've already told you, sunshine,' replied Ralph, sighing with good-natured tolerance. 'So the trespasser doesn't find out about our little business here.'

Annie stared at the trees. 'What if he's watching us now?' she asked.

'Doubt it, old thing,' said Ralph, grinning confidently. 'He'll be nicely tucked up in that old shack thing I saw him cobble together, making sure the bed bugs don't bite . . . '

Old shack thing. Mouse bit his lip indignantly, appalled by the idea that Ralph had spent the morning spying on him, no doubt watching for things to mock and ridicule. Until that moment, Mouse had been more pleased with his hut than anything else. Now it was as if he considered it properly for the first time for what it really was: an awkward jumble of twigs and mud. He felt a sense of humiliation.

Suddenly, all three Pendred children burst out laughing. Mouse was unable to hear their words but felt sure the joke was directed at him. Then they moved away into the double beam of the headlights, walking with the light forced against their backs, to one of the larger hummocks.

Mouse strained his eyes to see more, but it was so difficult. Everything was blurred. They appeared to be lifting something—a cover of some sort, and Ralph—was it Ralph?—was down on his knees, crawling forward into the earth, which appeared to devour him bit by bit.

Blinded by the intense light, Mouse could only see vague black shapes flitting before him. Occasionally one of the three returned carrying something, which was carefully placed in the back of the Land Rover. For an hour, Mouse lay flat to the grass. He lay so still that a hedgehog snuffled by without even noticing him. He grew uncomfortable. His muscles ached and he was more than relieved when Ralph called, 'Okay, old things, that's enough for tonight. Let's hit the track back home,' and all three Pendreds came drifting out of the white light like sleep-walkers.

Something undefined, but which had been puzzling Mouse for a long time, suddenly became clear as the three children clambered aboard the Land Rover. Who was driving it? As he watched, Ralph slipped in behind the steering wheel, the two others crushing in on the passenger side. Then Ralph started up the engine.

Just in time, Mouse lowered his face to prevent his eyes reflecting the headlights as the vehicle turned in a semi-circle. When he next lifted his head, the Land Rover had left the clearing and was climbing the steep slope out of the wood.

Back on his feet, Mouse wasted no time in investigating the mystery. Snatching up a clump of dry grass, he put a match to it; then with it fitfully glowing and crackling in his hand hurried across to the large hummock. Pulling aside the branches covering it, he held up the burning grass for a better look.

'A tunnel,' he whispered.

Its deepness surprised him. He saw grey bulging walls haphazardly shored with rough timber off-cuts and planks. But it was far deeper than his light could penetrate. In any case it fizzled and smokily went out.

Mouse lit another of his precious matches. The tunnel was like a gaping mouth into the ground. Like Ralph before him, he crawled forward, letting himself be swallowed.

From that first moment Mouse breathed in the earth's fusty odour, it brought to mind graveyards, worm ends, and long-locked rooms. The cold clay leeched warmth from his body; and broken stones thrusting through it were like bones in the skin of something long dead.

Despite the cold, Mouse found he was sweating. He lit a third match and was amazed to find light shining back at him, reflected by glass and fragments of pottery embedded in the tunnel's roof and sides. Ahead he saw the tunnel end in a blank wall where Ralph's small pick lay. To Mouse the secret of the tunnel was revealed. It was a mine—a bottle mine.

Suddenly he gave a cry and threw down the match that had burned to his fingers. In the earth's absolute darkness, he listened to his own breathing and wondered how to make use of his new discovery. Reluctantly he had to admit admiration for his rivals . . . for their mine . . . for their organization . . . and he pictured Ralph sitting confidently behind the wheel of the Land Rover. But Mouse was determined to make a stand.

Without benefit of light and using only his fingers, he prised as many bottles as he could from the walls and roof. (The clay's grip was as strong as a dead man's.) Then, dragging the bottles after him, he backed down the tunnel until the stars were once more overhead. Quickly he arranged the bottles about the mine's entrance with a dandelion flower in each one.

He couldn't resist another match simply to admire his joke. That ought to let 'em know two can play at this game, he thought, smiling to himself. Then, crawling into the tunnel a second time, he found the pick and claimed it for his own.

CHAPTER SIX

The Pendreds' retaliation came swiftly the following morning. With a terrific *thwack*, something struck hard against Mouse's hut as he lay sleeping there. Clumsily he stumbled to the doorway and peered out at the cold, grey, misty woodland. There was no one to be seen. He had just convinced himself that it was either a bird or squirrel, when a second lump of wet mud struck the hut inches above his head—clearly the intended target.

'Dirty trespasser!' screeched an angry high-pitched voice, which Mouse immediately recognized as belonging to the youngest of the three Pendreds.

'Hey, you—pack it up!' shouted Mouse as two more shots came in rapid succession, forcing him to shrug the old raincoat over his head and dart for cover.

The abuse and bombardment now gathered apace, while Mouse could feel his own anger rising inside him. What right had these Pendreds to call him names?—They didn't even know him. They had no right. He would stand for their rubbishing no more. With a cry of fury and his old coat flying behind him like a ragged war banner, he burst out to confront the enemy.

At once he glimpsed a flash of colour and saw Clyde break cover and go sprinting before him. At intervals, through the dense green, the blue jersey reappeared. Mouse was puzzled to hear giggles of delight. Soon the chase turned into a game of duck and weave through the wildest tracts of Jerusalem Wood. Here the smaller boy had the advantage over Mouse's speed and size. Yet bit by bit Mouse managed to close the gap and Clyde no longer giggled but bowed his head and drew his breath in gasps.

Mouse would have caught him, too, had not his trailing hem suddenly snagged on a thorny branch. As he crashed down, half trussed up in his own coat, his glance was momentarily directed backwards. His involuntary cry was cut dead as he struck the ground.

In that brief moment he caught sight of a red ball—a glowing red ball of fire; and he understood. Clyde was nothing more than a decoy to lure him away from his hut. Limping—swallowing down the sobs—he hobbled back over his tracks.

He heard the crackle of fire first; and, closer to, smoke wafted through the trees, patchily to begin with, then hot and gritty, blowing into his face. Intense heat came next, the fierceness of it finally stopping the boy dead in his tracks.

He arrived in time to witness his hut fold to the ground. No more than a bundle of ash and charred twigs. The span of the fire's life was as brief as it was fierce. Straight away it began dying back. The last few sparks flew up, the crackling grew more intermittent and the embers only glowed if stirred by the breeze. Surrounding trees were barely scorched.

To leave no doubt who had caused it, a skull and crossbones hung nearby. The message attached to it simply read:
'This is how to deal with dirty rotten thieves.
signed Ralph L. Pendred
Annie Pendred
Clyde Pendred (aged 8)'

Each name was written in a different hand.

Mouse tore the flag down and hurled it on to the fire.

As it burnt he made up his mind how to answer them.

His face smoke-blackened (except where the tears had left their tracks) he went down into the clearing. His manner was cold and purposeful. By gouging out struts and hammering with his heels he brought down the Pendreds' bottle mine. Then he turned and went running back into the trees.

It was early evening when the Pendreds discovered what he had done. Ralph stood amongst the ruins, thoughtfully chewing a match. Annie and Clyde watched him closely. Clyde had an irritating sniff.

Ralph shook his head. Clearly matters had got out of hand, he never intended they should go this far. With a branch he poked through the landslip pulling out newly exposed bottles that shone through the broken earth. He picked his way with extreme care so as not to muddy his highly-polished brogues. Unlike Annie and Clyde he was unarmed. A sheath knife hung from Annie's leather belt and in her hand she carried a stick taller than herself; her readiness to do battle shown by the camouflaged jacket she wore. Clyde, on the other hand, trusted to his catapult. He kept snapping its elastic until Annie wanted to tell him to shut up but was afraid she might ruin the solemness of the moment.

Then, as they watched, Annie and her brother noticed Ralph's eyes suddenly fixed upon something behind them. He spat out the match and his expression hardened. Slowly they turned to follow his stare.

'It's the dirty mine wrecker,' hissed Clyde.

The Pendred gang glared poisonously at Mouse as he emerged from the trees. Calmly he came forward, edging his way bit by bit, but his course always straight and always towards them. On both sides curiosity was strong. Mouse was a creature of mystery. He sensed it in himself. After three days in the same clothes, eating sparsely and sleeping rough he resembled something wild and unpredictable. Clyde backed towards Annie as if a big dog were approaching.

'You burnt down my hut!' bellowed Mouse, screwing up his face and making his hands into tight fists. 'You . . . you . . . you 'ad no right!'

'Listen, pal,' said Ralph sourly, jabbing at the air with a finger. 'You did this to our mine.'

'Smelly ol' trespasser!' shouted Clyde.

Mouse ran forward as if to knock him down, then stopped. 'You started it! You declared war first!' His voice was thick with emotion.

Ralph took a step towards him; he was smooth, confident, and calm: 'You made your point, pal. You said what you wanted to say. Best you run along now. Go back to where you came from. There was no trouble here until you—'

His sentence went unfinished. Mouse, head down, gasping and crying, flung himself at the older boy, never noticing the glancing blow from Annie's stick. Taken by surprise, Ralph was dragged off his feet, muddying his expensive tweed jacket and fine leather shoes.

Mouse, beyond reason, fought with flailing arms, leaving himself open to one of Ralph's occasional well-aimed punches. But Mouse felt no pain—nothing—at least not until later. He was crying and babbling—spilling out utter nonsense. Annie and Clyde surged angrily around him, shouting and pulling at his hair and clothes. Blows from hands and sticks seemed to drop from the sky.

Pinned down beneath him where he fell, Ralph's actions were at first defensive. But as he was more and more provoked and Mouse—exhausted by hunger—began to weaken, the bigger boy slowly overcame him. Every time his fist struck there was an awful crack as if the skinny kid would shatter like brittle glass.

Three successive times Ralph struck him in the face. Mouse toppled backwards with a cry, his hair thickening with mud as he slithered down the slope. Before he could rise, Ralph fell upon him. Mouse coughed out his breath.

'Had enough punishment, pal?' Ralph growled through his teeth. 'You ready to throw in the towel yet?'

Mouse quivered with sobs, unable to make a reply.

Slowly and with distaste, Ralph clambered off him. He scowled to see his clothes muddied, scratching at the mud with a finger nail.

Annie and Clyde stood in silence. They peered down at Mouse, not with pity, but in curiosity.

'Come on,' snapped Ralph.

The gang shuffled away behind him. At the last moment Annie turned back. Mouse hadn't moved. His chest heaved and his face lay hidden beneath the crook of his elbow.

'Ralph,' she said, chewing her bottom lip, 'I think you may have hurt him. Really. I think you have.'

'He started it,' said Clyde.

'I didn't want to fight him anyway,' said Ralph. 'He struck the first blow. He forced me—I had to defend myself.'

'Still,' persisted Annie, 'he might be hurt badly.' She frowned. 'It wouldn't be right just leaving him there.'

They watched, waiting for Mouse to stir. When he didn't Ralph sighed heavily.

'Come on,' he said. 'We'd better see what damage is done.'

They crept back as if Mouse might explode

in their faces like a bomb. His mouth hung open and there was blood on his teeth. Once more Annie and Clyde found themselves drawn by curiosity. They stared at Mouse, then at Ralph, who said somewhat briskly, 'Come on, pal. Up you get.'

'W-why?' sniffed Mouse after a long silence. 'I w-wanna st-stay here till I d-die.'

Ralph glanced at the ground. Finding a patch of clean grass he sat down beside him.

'Look here, sunshine, I didn't want to squash you. Truly. I've nothing against you personally. Don't even know you. So please stop crying . . . Tell you what, we'll give you a lift to the road. How about that? You can make your own way home.'

'What h-home?' came the bitter reply and with his arm clamped over his face, Mouse's story poured out of him, punctuated only by swallows and sobs. 'And now,' he finished, 'I g-got nowhere t'go. You b-burnt down m-my hut.'

Ralph looked shamefaced. 'Sorry, pal,' he shrugged. 'How were we to know?'

'You were just a grubby little thief and trespasser to us,' piped up Clyde unhelpfully. 'We thought you were trying to steal our mine.'

'I d-didn't know you were here. I c-came looking for old b-bottles—you know—like bburied treasure.'

His words, sounding mildly ridiculous, caused Annie to give a nervous snort. Ralph narrowed his eyes at her.

'Really sorry, pal,' he said, his voice softening. 'Truly I am. But think how it looked to us. This stranger just turns up and suddenly it seems like he's trying to muscle in on our patch. We couldn't let you get away with that, now could we?'

Mouse lamely shook his head in grudging agreement.

'Listen on, sunshine,' continued Ralph. 'Perhaps there is something we can do for you.'

Mouse heard Ralph usher his gang away then, at a distance, he heard their muttered voices.

'Oh no, Ralph!' Annie suddenly blurted out. 'What a thing to ask. He's a scruffy little tyke. He smells. Give him some money so he goes away and leaves us alone.'

'But where will he go, old thing?' asked Ralph patiently. 'You heard what he told us. He's got nowhere. Absolutely nowhere.'

'What if we don't like him?' demanded Clyde bluntly.

'Well, he doesn't seem such a bad sort—not once you scrape the dirt away. Look on him as an extra pair of hands. He's already proved that he can be resourceful. I think we can do something with him. Truly I do.'

By this time Mouse was listening so intently he forgot to sob. He had no idea what Ralph was suggesting but Annie sounded sulky and resentful, and Clyde, being Clyde, simply prattled on. Eventually, Ralph talked both round to his view as, of course, he knew he would.

Mouse heard the step of his heavy brogues. A strong hand took his arm and Mouse blinked up at the sky, ashamed of his red, tear-stained eyes.

'Listen, sunshine,' said Ralph, squatting down on his haunches, 'we've decided to let you in. Join our gang. But first you must swear never to tell a living soul about what goes on here. We don't want our wood crawling with bottle collectors. So do you swear?'

Mouse nodded his head.

'He has to say it,' said Annie darkly.

'I swear,' said Mouse. 'Cross my heart and hope t'die.'

'Now he has to spit to seal it.'

Propping himself up on an elbow, Mouse dribbled some saliva; he saw blood mixed with it.

'Huh!' said Annie unimpressed. Turning away, she tossed her hair over her shoulder.

With friendly roughness Ralph bundled

Mouse to his feet, vigorously shaking him by the hand. Mouse looked bemused. When Ralph placed a hand on his shoulder to guide him away Mouse recoiled.

'Where you taking me?' he demanded.

'Can't have you sleeping rough, sunshine,' smiled Ralph. 'Not now you're one of us. How do you fancy bunking down in a proper bed for a change? We know just the place.'

CHAPTER SEVEN

The Land Rover was parked off the track.
Close to, it appeared old and battered, yet for
Mouse this made it no less desirable. The
driver's door was painted a different tone of
green and a deep crack divided the windscreen in two. The body was dented and
scratched and rust was beginning to bubble
beneath the paintwork.

'This really yours?' asked Mouse, unable to
hide his admiration.

'Every last bolt of her,' replied Ralph,
smiling proudly as he ran his hand along the
vehicle's wing. 'Bought her from Old Timson
the farmer—straight cash from our profits. He
wanted a lot more, of course, but I haggled
and brought the price down. I think he was
astounded by my cheek.'

He opened the passenger door.

'It's a proper work-horse, you know,' he
went on, 'and saves us a lot of backache when

shifting bottles. Annie wanted to give it a name, but you can't give working machines names. Besides it's too babyish. Oh, and listen, sunshine, nobody else knows about it so best you don't mention it, either.'

Mouse nodded. 'Ain' it against the law?' he asked.

'*Isn't it*,' corrected Ralph with the patient tone of a teacher. He shook his head. 'We use it mostly after dark and never on the roads, which can be a bit of a pain. The rest of the time it's hidden away. Now come on, be a good chap and hop in. I may have taught myself but I'm a fairly good driver.'

Inside, the leather seats were worn and the floor littered with sweet wrappers and cans. Mouse's eyes immediately fell upon a bar of half-eaten chocolate and they couldn't stop straying back to it. He had forgotten his empty stomach. Now, reminded of it, the hunger pangs increased.

Ralph grinned at him then started up the engine. His seat was pushed as far forward as it would go and he had to sit on two cushions to obtain a driving view. The remaining seat was uncomfortably shared by the others, with Clyde settling himself like an overgrown baby on Annie's lap. To Mouse's surprise neither one showed the slightest embarrassment at the arrangement, Clyde happily sucking his thumb and Annie hugging him to her.

However, should her arm happen to brush against Mouse, she pointedly withdrew it, with a sharp intake of breath. Mouse was miserably aware of his own filthy condition, but Annie brought the fact home by winding down the window and thrusting out her head. She even avoided glancing in his direction.

Slowly the Land Rover bumped its way along the woodland track. The undergrowth grew less densely here and single graceful ferns arched over in the headlights. Mouse watched in silence over a spare wheel bolted to the bonnet.

Beyond Jerusalem Wood lay open fields and the chance for Ralph to use the accelerator. He may have been trying to impress Mouse because, after one particularly severe jolt, Annie rounded on him and snapped, 'That's enough, Ralph!'

A fresh breeze swirled into the cab, flicking her hair into Mouse's face. If she realized, she didn't care, choosing to stare vacantly out of the side window at empty fields.

As Ralph had said, they relied on none of the country lanes, and the way they dealt with the many field-gates had grown into a precise art. Seeing one loom up in the distance, Ralph would say, 'Go, Clyde!' and slow the Land Rover to a crawl. Thereupon Clyde would scramble out and run before them in the headlights. He'd ride upon the gate as it swung open, riding it shut again afterwards. The Land Rover never stopped and when Clyde was back inside the cab Ralph was sure to roar with laughter before announcing a time from an expensive gold watch. 'Twenty-five seconds . . . ' or 'Thirty-eight seconds . . . ' adding, 'Improving, Clyde . . . Improving,' or 'Getting tired, sunshine.'

Presently they reached an overgrown track and when Ralph bumped up on to it, Mouse saw the big grey hall standing squarely before them and his mouth dropped open.

'You live there?'

This greatly amused Ralph. 'No,' he grinned. 'But I daresay I'll probably live in something like it one day.'

'So where *do* you live?' asked Mouse.

Ralph shrugged vaguely. 'Oh, away in the next village.'

'Coldby?'

'Huh? Oh no. Nowhere special.'

Mouse gained the impression that Ralph wanted to pass over the question, so he turned his attention to the hall.

'Ralph,' he began hesitantly, 'I don't know if I should be going there. You see I—'

'You nicked stuff from the garden!' snapped Annie, suddenly turning her glare on him.

'My, we are surprised!'

'I 'ad to,' cried Mouse. 'Would it please you if I starved?'

Ralph laughed and said, 'All right, Mouse, no need to rant on.' He nodded at the hall. 'The old boy who lives up there is very protective of his vegetable garden. He's a bit . . . well . . . a bit peculiar when it comes to food. As a matter of fact he's a pretty strange old boy all round. But quite harmless. He's from Poland and sometimes, to hear him go on, you'd think the Second World War was still taking place. Just you leave all the talking to me.'

'But . . . but . . . he shot at me—with a gun!'

Clyde giggled. 'Don't worry,' he said. 'Joe's a rubbish shot. He couldn't hit an elephant.'

Then with a squeal of brakes they were there.

His three companions climbed down from the cab at once. Mouse followed with reluctance. The Pendreds were so at ease that Mouse guessed they were probably frequent visitors there. Ralph ran up the crumbling steps to beat upon the door.

'Come on, Joe, it's us!' he called. 'Come on, squire—open up! Can't hang about all night, you know.'

'Go easy, Ralph,' whispered Annie. 'You'll scare him.'

'All right, Annie old thing, I know what I'm doing,' said Ralph.

Five minutes of door banging followed until finally the door creaked open to the width of an inch. Through the gap peered the frightened face of an old man. He clutched an oil lamp before him and its light, cast upwards, exaggerated his sagging skin and hollow eyes.

'Ya?' he demanded. 'Vhat iz et you vant?' He pulled the filthy dressing gown across his chest. 'Et damn late, you kno'. Damn late.' He sounded angry and afraid.

Once the door was open Ralph calmly swept inside. 'Friend, Joe,' he said smoothly. 'It's me—Ralph.'

'I know damn vell who et iz!' The old man's voice seemed to break. 'Vhy you com', Ral'h?' he pleaded. 'Vhy? Don't you know vhat damn o'clock et iz?'

'Emergency, Joe,' explained Ralph, gesturing at Mouse. 'We have . . . er . . . a refugee and he needs a safe house. Be a sport, Joe. Let him hole up with you for a few days.'

Joe lifted his lamp to study the dirty, ragged child who nervously edged through the doorway. He could indeed be a refugee. Joe gazed at him for a long time.

'Who after you, boy?' he asked in a sorrowful voice. 'Da Nazis?—Thoze damn

Communiztz? You tell me who et iz.'

'I . . . I don't know,' shrugged Mouse, meaning he had no idea what Joe was talking about.

'Ya—both az damn bad,' agreed the old man, vigorously nodding his head. 'I daresay you stop vith me. Few dayz, mind. I not vish to be damn caught and shot. Nazis and Communiztz. Huh! Iv et pleazes God may they shoot each other. And you, boy, you listen vhen Joseph Dabrowski speakz: I have no food to give you. You un'erstand my talk, boy? No food.'

'Don't worry, Joe,' said Ralph with a grin. 'We'll feed him.'

As he and Joe haggled over the arrangements, Mouse let his eyes wander over the hallway. From where he stood he had no real measure of its depth, but felt sure if he shouted out his name the echo would return from high up in the house. The squalor all around amazed him. The chequered tiled floor was sticky with grime, elegant chairs stood swamped beneath newspapers, and unopened mail made a drift under the brass letter box. Like the lamp of some ancient galleon, a great cobwebby lantern came out of the gloom on a heavy metal chain. When last it was bright, thought Mouse, pictures must have hung on the walls instead of the unfaded patches that were there now, showing where they had been. Then he noticed, by a stack of firewood, a shabby stuffed bear, looking pathetic and mildly ridiculous. Clyde caught him looking at it and grinned, but Mouse thought it sad.

A movement focused his attention. A door had opened and a cat came strolling out, his tail in the air like a question-mark.

'Napoleon!' cried Clyde, leaping after the creature which, like his namesake, decided to retreat—into the room from which he had just appeared.

The boy pursued him there.

Joe, greatly agitated, pulled his greasy dressing gown tightly to his neck. 'You com' back, boy!' he called, scuttling after him.

Ralph whispered into Mouse's ear, 'The old boy has the whole house to himself, but only lives in a few rooms downstairs. Come see.' His tone sounded inviting. But when Mouse showed no sign of moving, Ralph seized his arm and dragged him along.

Beyond the door lay a long, tall, narrow room where the gloom was intense and the smell was of damp plaster, despite a fire in the grate. The curtains were drawn, their rotting linings hanging in threads; and a smashed chandelier from the ornate ceiling sat in a tarnished heap in a chair. The remaining furniture was covered in dust sheets. Then Mouse noticed the tins of food. They cluttered every available ledge and were piled up on the tables. They lurked half concealed under fringed covers, spilled out from behind dust sheets and filled cardboard boxes in the alcoves. Tinned tomatoes, beans, sardines, spam, rice pudding . . . Some so old that they were covered in thick dust or spotted with rust; some slowly slipping off their mouldering labels.

Mouse picked up an ancient tin of corned beef and immediately Joe was before him, snatching it out of his hands and slamming it back down as if it were a chess piece in a game he was playing.

'I tell you, boy,' he said, bristling with anger, 'Joseph Dabrowski have no food to share. He save theze zo he not go hungry in old age.'

'Don't get angry, Joe,' pleaded Annie softly.

'Pah!' he snorted.

Ralph carelessly cast himself into a broken-backed chair. 'Had a tough time back in Poland, didn't you, Joe?' He was speaking to the old man but explaining to Mouse. 'Went without in the bad old days of the war, isn't that right, you poor old thing?'

The old man nodded. 'First Nazis they com', then Communiztz. Damn hard. *You* vill never know,' he spoke bitterly. 'Cold . . . cold and da hunger. Ha, real nightmare hunger.

Vhen da skin iz pinching your damn bonez.'

Mouse looked at him, not knowing what to say.

Ralph said, 'Don't fret, Joe. We'll take care of our little refugee here. Didn't I promise we would?' He rose to his feet. 'I'll show him to a room, eh, Joe? We'll give him the one right at the top of the house so he can keep watch and raise the alarm if the enemy comes.'

'Do vhat you vish,' said the old man crustily. He fumbled his way to a group of medicine bottles, tapped two tablets into his palm and gulped them down dry, his throat as leathery and pouched as a lizard's.

Closing the door on him, Ralph grinned. 'I told you Joe would be a piece of cake,' he said. 'He just needed a little talking round, that's all.'

'The way you spoke to him,' said Mouse, 'anyone would have thought this house belonged t'you.'

Ralph winked.

Now with Annie and Clyde falling in behind, he led Mouse by candlelight up the grand staircase. Bare boards rang hollow beneath their feet and, in places, sections of elegant lyre-shaped banister had crumbled away. The steps themselves were an obstacle course of broken chairs, rolled up rugs and empty tea-chests, which together created the impression that the house had just been looted.

At the third landing Ralph paused, a thoughtful expression on his face. Then he said, 'Come with me, Mouse, I want to show you something.'

'Please, Ralph!' cried Annie at once. 'You're giving away too many of our secrets.'

'So, a few more really won't matter,' replied Ralph dismissively and, strolling up to a door, threw it open.

Mouse followed him through and immediately burst out laughing with delight.

Grubby floorboards shone like liquid, covered as they were in green glass of every shade. Green Victorian beer bottles with embossed letters and logos stood alongside green poison bottles especially ribbed to warn the blind; and little green ornamental jars shaped like cottages and snail shells; and green lemonade bottles with marbles in their necks; and medicine bottles; and bottles mysteriously shaped or decorated; and plain bottles of every size, alike in one respect only—the colour of their glass.

Mouse picked up the nearest glass object and read aloud, 'Warner's safe kidney and liver cure.'

He laughed again.

By moonlight the room shimmered and

gleamed, alive in a way which was almost sinister. Quite abruptly Mouse stopped laughing and set the bottle down again.

But other doors were being opened for him into new rooms. Rooms of blue glass, yellow glass, and brown glass. One room contained a few rare pieces of red and pink glass; another room housed black whisky bottles and gin bottles grimly shaped like coffins. Clear and opaque glassware filled several rooms by themselves, and Mouse carefully picked his way between wide-necked milk bottles, baby feeders, soda syphons, and fairy lights. Yet another room was devoted to a wide variety of pottery objects: ginger-beer bottles, clay pipe bowls, doll heads, cream jugs, stone hot-water bottles, and pot lids elaborately advertising such things as bears' grease, toothpaste, and gentleman's relish. The final room contained a table and lots of cardboard boxes, and was where the muddy, newly excavated objects waited to be washed and sorted.

'Doesn't Joe mind you using his house like this?' asked Mouse as Ralph ushered him out and closed the door.

'Joe's scared of air raids so he never comes upstairs,' replied Ralph, pausing to consider a question he had obviously never considered before, 'so I can't rightly say he doesn't mind—but what he never finds out about can't possibly harm him, can it? Besides, I think he grudgingly likes having us Pendreds here—we're a bit of company for him. Otherwise all he has is his cat.'

'And we do buy him presents,' chimed in Clyde. 'He likes tins of pineapple chunks and chocolate biscuits. Sometimes he eats them, sometimes he adds them to his collection.'

Talk of food reminded Mouse of his own hunger. Ralph noticed and said, 'Come on, sunshine. We'll show you to a room and get you fixed up.'

Mouse nodded eagerly.

He was taken a floor higher to a small irregular-shaped room tucked away just beneath the eaves. Its rose-bud patterned wallpaper was peeling; and musty brown damp patches recalled to mind indistinct maps of countries and continents. There was a large brass bed but no other furniture.

Annie lit some candles. She knew her way around the room so well it could have been her own. A little cast-iron fireplace lay ready for lighting. Kneeling down, Annie put her candle to the kindling wood and bright yellow light fell across her pale skin.

Mouse glanced back at her as he followed Ralph into a yet still smaller room behind the bed. Its door was so low it could have been made for a child. The room had no window and contained only an ancient sink. Ralph turned on a tap. Nothing happened, except a distant drumming from the pipes.

'The pressure's quite low at the top of the house,' he explained. 'You'll find the water a little yellow when it eventually comes through. But it's perfectly safe.'

A slither of soap was pressed into Mouse's grubby hand and clean clothes rooted out for him from the cupboard beneath the sink.

'There you go,' said Ralph, carelessly tossing them at Mouse. 'These are mine. They may be on the large size for you, but at least they're clean.'

Ten minutes later, when Mouse returned to the bedroom, he looked so different that Annie and Clyde, sprawling on the bed, sat up and stared at him as if he were someone they had never set eyes on before. Ralph, frying-pan in hand, straightened up, grinning his approval. He gestured at the four beefburgers in the pan which he was cooking over the fire, holding the metal handle with a rag to stop it burning him.

'Supper,' he announced grandly. Mouse sniffed long and deep, believing he had never smelt anything so delicious. He begged Ralph to stop wasting time and finish the job.

'Here,' said Annie coldly. 'If you're so hungry . . .'

She threw a packet of sliced bread at him. There was also a whole tray of cola from which he was expected to help himself. But it was food his stomach craved. So ravenously hungry was he that he started picking at the dry bread. He must have made a pig of himself, for he caught sight of Annie watching him with an expression of utter disgust. Attempting to apologize, he found his mouth stuffed full of bread.

'Yuk!' said Annie, turning away with a superior toss of her head.

'There you go, sunshine,' said Ralph, handing Mouse a fork and the frying-pan to eat from. 'Scoff up. There's plenty more where these come from.'

CHAPTER EIGHT

Mouse awoke about midday unable to recall the exact moment he put down his head to sleep. He remembered the food lying as heavy as stones in his stomach and fighting against an overwhelming sense of weariness. It was like an ache. He had slept long and deep. Now awake and refreshed he stretched himself on the lumpy goose-feather mattress, beneath a pile of coats that covered him, keeping him warm.

Minutes later he heard whistling on the stairs and Ralph burst in. He was wearing a panama hat and chewing a matchstick which he lazily rolled back and forth across his mouth.

'Morning, Mouse,' he said brightly.

He set a Dundee marmalade jar brimming with white daisies on the mantel over the fireplace then, indicating be patient a moment longer, went from the room, returning shortly after clutching a great many carrier-bags.

'I've been shopping,' he said.

Mouse couldn't believe his generosity. Everything was for him. Ralph threw the bags on the end of the bed and together they made quite a pile. Poor Mouse was moved to tears. He couldn't stop saying 'Thank you, Ralph. Thank you,' over and over again.

It seemed that Ralph had thought of everything from toothpaste to handkerchiefs; while clothing was usefully provided in pairs. At first Mouse delighted in feeling each item in turn, crackling the expensive cellophane packaging. Never before had he received so many brand-new things—certainly not at Christmas or on his birthday. At least, not in recent years.

'I took your sizes from the labels in your old clothes,' said Ralph, stretching himself across the bed like a cat. 'If I were you, sunshine, I'd throw that old stuff away.'

'What?'

'Burn it,' said Ralph. 'Start afresh.'

The notion that he could do so thrilled Mouse. He could make a clean break with the past.

Naturally he grew eager to try everything on; so Ralph held a flaking mirror while he admired himself from every angle. Mouse saw at once that he resembled a smaller, self-conscious version of Ralph, except his tweed jacket and brogues weren't quite the same top - notch quality as those Ralph wore. Still, if he was an incomplete copy of Ralph, so what? Mouse was more than happy to be the shadow of such an original.

Speaking solemnly he said, 'I'll take care of everything, Ralph. Promise.'

Ralph shrugged as if to say that was for Mouse to decide.

Later—like brothers—as they clattered down the stairs, Joe stuck his head out of the door. He peered at Mouse, unsure whether he was the same boy who had arrived the previous night. He sniffed like an old badger and backed away into his den. Ralph looked at Mouse and they both burst out laughing.

Outside, the Land Rover stood on the gravel.

'Want a go?' asked Ralph, dangling the keys before Mouse's face.

'Me?'

'Why not?' said Ralph. He opened the driver's door and ushered Mouse in. 'I've just decided that I'm going to teach you to drive.'

A long time was spent patiently explaining about the different pedals and gears and how to steer. Mouse started and stalled several times, before the vehicle juddered forward into a smoother ride. *Twenty miles an hour!*

And to Mouse the world was racing by. Turning to Ralph he giggled with nervous excitement and momentarily lost control. Ralph grabbed the wheel and steadied its course.

Wisely, perhaps, he decided to end Mouse's first lesson here. He took over the controls saying, 'How about I give you a tour—show you around for a bit. You can be the lookout.'

'What for?'

'Angry farmers,' replied Ralph. 'They don't take too kindly to us crossing their land.'

Mouse was happy to do anything Ralph suggested and whenever they reached a gate he dashed out to open it because he didn't want to keep Ralph waiting.

'Thanks, sunshine,' said Ralph, each time flashing a smile at his willing assistant.

He parked the Land Rover at the edge of Jerusalem Wood and, following a rabbit track, they made their way to its centre. It turned out that Ralph was extremely knowledgeable about country matters. He knew the names of trees, the different wild flowers, and could predict the weather from clouds. He also spoke at length about glass and bottles. He had made them his special study and now, speaking of them to Mouse, he brought their history alive like an incredible story . . .

Glass existed in the world before dinosaurs. It was a chance-made thing. Created when lightning struck the shores of the first oceans. Extreme heat forged sand grains into delicate fingers of glass which geologists call fulgurites.

Perhaps this natural phenomenon was observed in Egypt or Mesopotamia nearly four thousand years ago by men who copied the process to make glass of their own. Even today the basic ingredients remain unchanged. Sand and great heat.

From the Middle East the art of glass making spread. In all ancient civilizations it played a part. The Romans produced it for every level of society. Then came the Dark Ages when glass making was all but forgotten and chieftains slurped mead from lumpy clay pots in huts they called palaces with pigs about their thrones.

The darkness lasted until dazzlingly illuminated by the great church builders, their windows glowing as the sun rose, flooding the cathedrals and abbeys with pools of colour. Their work was little less than magic in an age that forbade magic; and like alchemists the glass-makers carefully added their potions and powders. Copper for reds, nickel for purples, cobalt for blues, chromium for greens, iron for yellows . . . In the huddle of the city around, windows were little more than slots and holes, yet these men had faith enough in God and glass to build windows that soared up to the vaults.

For centuries after, only the well-to-do could afford glass. Governments taxed it so it remained a luxury. But a tax on glass also meant a tax on windows; and brick-layers found profit at the glaziers' expense as scores of windows in buildings, from the grandest hall to the most tumble-down cottage, were bricked up to escape its burden. Finally the government gave in to the demand for cheap glass and, by the end of the nineteenth century, beer was available in as many shaped bottles as there were breweries.

This was the true age of glass; the great Victorian engineers cherished it as much as steam engines and suspension bridges. They domed corn exchanges and libraries with it; glass-canopied the metropolitan railway stations; and palaces of crystal displayed every wonder of the day. But these engineers were improvers, too, and, taking the humble bottle, they put their minds to the perfect stopper and came up with a variety of ingenious inventions. The internal screw stopper appeared in 1871, the swing stopper in 1875, and the crown cork in 1892. Best of all was Hiram Codd's globe-stopper—favoured by small boys for the marble it contained.

And what was commonplace and throwaway to Victorian schoolboys was now valuable and sought after in this present plastic age.

Ralph said rarer bottles could be worth hundreds of pounds—even if they contained nothing.

Mouse nodded. He felt he contained nothing. Empty beside Ralph who brimmed with knowledge.

By now they had reached the old lake site, and Ralph revealed that the Pendreds had a name for their bottle mine, a secret name he wanted Mouse to know. It was called the Grub-Out.

'Pretty good name, don't you think?' said Ralph.

On hearing this and seeing the extent of his own vandalism to it, Mouse grew ashamed and began to stammer apologies.

'Forget it, Mouse,' said Ralph with a wave of his hand. 'After all, we did burn your hut. And rather good it was, too. I bet it was waterproof.'

'I 'spect it was,' replied Mouse affecting modesty, but glowing with pride.

'Actually,' said Ralph, 'I think you did us a favour when you flattened the Grub-Out.'

'I did?' said Mouse, astonished.

Ralph nodded. 'It was about exhausted. Besides, we've had other mines, it's not our first. Let me see, before the Grub-Out there was the Slime Pit and before that there was the Claggie. You get quite attached to them, you know. The Grub-Out never was up to much. It's in the wrong place.'

'You thinking of digging a fourth mine?' asked Mouse. 'I mean, I'd like t'help if—'

'We have a fourth mine already,' said Ralph. He pointed. 'Over there on the other side. We boarded it up and hid it so well you never found it. We even disguised its spoil heaps by planting them with wild flowers. The Big Daddy was dug before any of the other three—that's what we christened it. The Big Daddy. It's where we found our oldest and most valuable bottles.'

Mouse couldn't avoid asking the obvious question: 'So why did you shut it up?'

Ralph frowned. 'You see where it is, how near to the stream? Sometimes water gets in and the walls can be unsafe if they're not properly shored up. However—' his expression quickly brightened, 'with the two of us working together, we could make a go of it. It'll be well worth our while, Mouse. Truly.'

'Anything you say, Ralph.'

'Good man.'

That night Ralph decreed a feast. When the moon was risen he drove to Jerusalem Wood and once there everyone scurried about collecting sticks for a fire.

Cooking was a noisy haphazard affair which Mouse soon learnt was the Pendred way of doing things. Chops went on spits, eggs and bacon sizzled in the frying-pan, and cans of tomatoes and baked beans—their lids jaggedly ripped open—absorbed heat at the fire's edge. Luckily Annie had remembered the camping kettle, so they could boil up for tea, afterwards drinking from huge striped mugs that needed both hands to lift.

Smoke swirled, wood crackled, and the Land Rover's headlights poured steadily through the trees. It was perfect, thought Mouse, contentedly lying back on the damp earth to stare up at the moon through a criss-cross of black branches . . . Or at least would be but for one small thing. Annie. Why couldn't she try to like him a little? If she spoke to him—which she did only when necessary—it was with a hostile little word, or else took the form of a barbed command or cold request.

In the end, Mouse decided to take his courage in both hands and strike up a conversation with her.

'Err-umm,' he began unpromisingly. 'Ralph

sh-showed me all your bottle mines today. He t-told me their names.'

Annie grunted; she didn't look at him. 'I suppose you know all our secrets now,' she said.

'Don't worry,' said Mouse quickly, 'I'll not tell anyone.'

'Bet you would under torture,' said Clyde. He was sitting on a log, his fingers thrust into a jar of chutney.

'Not for a long time,' admitted Mouse after briefly giving the matter some thought.

Annie flicked back her hair.

Mouse saw he had made no impression whatsoever. Desperate to break the silence he spoke again, his words tumbling out in a breathless rush. 'Ralph's keen to start digging in the Big Daddy again. Says that's where we can make us some real money.'

This time he did engage her interest, although not in the way he had hoped. The girl's dark eyes flashed angrily at him. Then she turned to Ralph.

'Is this true, Ralph? Are you really opening up the Big Daddy again? Tell me he's lying!'

'It has crossed my mind,' said Ralph, slowly putting down his plate. 'No need for you to fret about it, old thing.'

'But it's too dangerous,' fumed Annie.

'Not with care.'

'Look at this . . .' Annie turned to Mouse and pulled back her sleeve. A long, pale scar ran along her sunburnt arm. 'I did that in the Big Daddy. The sides gave way. I could have been killed.'

'You exaggerate, Annie. You had a nasty scratch and it shook you up. It won't happen again.' Ralph smiled at Mouse. 'We think opening the Big Daddy is a good idea—don't we, Mouse?'

'Er . . . yes, Ralph.'

Annie glared at Mouse so contemptuously that he was forced to turn away.

CHAPTER NINE

Work on the Big Daddy commenced the next day. Ralph loaded planks and nails into the back of the Land Rover.

Following Annie's accident, the Big Daddy was blocked off with boards and covered with soil for the weeds to colonize. Ralph was right: Mouse would never have found it—not in a hundred years.

They stood back to let Ralph take a good swing at the boards with a sledgehammer, then crowded forward, curious to peer into the jagged hole he had made. They saw a dismal sight. Water dripped steadily from the roof, forming deep puddles of black scummy water. In places the earth's pressure had caused the mud to ooze through the shored walls, blocking the mine almost to its roof.

When the opening was large enough Ralph went in, passing back buckets of black liquid earth. It was a relentlessly monotonous chore, yet before the day was out everyone had done a stint at it. No one refused or complained. It was August—high summer, the trees becalmed by the intense heat—yet after half an hour of slithering on their bellies in the filth and dark, each one came up cold and miserable. Ralph said they ought to have a cauldron of soup continuously simmering away. Something to warm them, which they could top up with vegetables whenever required.

Ralph thought of everything. He even wore a proper miner's helmet with a lamp on top and, unlike the others, managed never to get mud on his face. Before she went down, Annie tucked her long hair into a peaked cap. It suited her, but made her features appear much sharper. Mouse watched as she smoothed away the last few strands of hair. He thought he did so secretly, until suddenly she rounded on him.

'I'm not scared, you know,' she said proudly and Mouse felt his face blush.

In the days following, Mouse came to believe the Big Daddy possessed a wilful, malicious life of its own, quite unlike the Grub-Out. That was a dead thing—hewn out of lifeless clay. The Big Daddy, on the other hand, split planks, bowed sides and flooded the hollows as soon as they were drained. Its fury was blind and unrelenting; and it even breathed out its own particular odour—a mixture of mould and decay—which hung about their clothes and hair even after a thorough washing.

A week was spent mending the damage. Then the first bottles began to show—some curiously shaped things, aptly called onion bottles. Ralph said they were highly prized by collectors, provided they were in mint condition. However, for every good bottle brought into the light, there were the smashed remains of countless others and Mouse bloodied his hands on the broken pieces.

Later he discovered what became of the bottles and other objects once washed and sorted. He met Bart, a tall, loose-limbed fellow with tangled hair down his back and an untrimmed moustache. Every Friday morning, Bart came to a field where Ralph conducted business with him from the back of the Land Rover. Some hard bartering took place, with Ralph more than able to stand his ground. Commoner pieces were sold in boxed lots (there was a general demand for old bottles amongst antique shops). Rarer or more distinctive finds were sold individually.

'You're robbing me, man! You're robbing me!' Bart would exclaim, excitedly waving his arms in the air. But it was all part of the act;

played with equal vigour by Ralph in his deerstalker hat and embroidered waistcoat. Like a sword he brandished a rolled-up copy of the latest *Bottles and Relics News*; while his chief tactic was to quote its prices as if fixed like a law. Bart replied, as Bart always did, by slapping his forehead and crying, 'You're taking my life's blood, man!'

After the shouting, a fat roll of money changed hands, then Bart and Ralph went their separate ways, and always on the friendliest of terms.

Ralph managed all financial matters and, as controller of the purse strings, took to buying extravagant presents.

'Saw this,' he would announce in his nonchalant way or with a dismissive sweep of his hand, 'and immediately thought of you, sunshine. Hope you like it.' And of course they always did.

If it occurred to the other three that the money Ralph squandered rightfully belonged to all of them, it was never mentioned. As a group they unquestioningly accepted Ralph's decisions; so when he said he wanted to be a millionaire by the time he was twenty, each one wondered how he could play his part in helping him. Certainly Mouse would have done anything for Ralph. His own happiness was tied to Ralph's well-being.

And all the time, Mouse continued living at Coldby Hall: which meant the problem of Joe downstairs . . .

'Vhat! That damn boy—he still here!' he'd come out of his door every few days to bellow. 'He get me shot. They stand me 'gainzt a vall and bang-bang, no more Joseph Dabrowski!'

'But he's the same as you, Joe,' Ralph remonstrated. 'He's a refugee, old thing.'

'I no care! Damn Nazis! Damn Communiztz! They shoot me iv they find da boy. He muzt go. Out! By noon ov thiz day!'

At first Mouse was alarmed by these threats, but soon realized that Joe's rages might be bought off with a simple gift—a packet of cigarettes, a couple of magazines, some cat food for Napoleon . . . And this was precisely the point of them. Ralph knew perfectly well how the old man worked and was kind, and mocking, and condescending towards him, encouraging Mouse to be the same. Mouse could never quite manage it. He was not Ralph.

For Mouse, the best times were the evenings after work was done, when they were free to play games—elaborate games invented by Ralph, who possessed a genius for making them up. A single game was quite capable of lasting for hours and since it was rare for the

Pendreds to leave before ten o'clock, Mouse grew all the more inquisitive about their home life. He no longer questioned Ralph, of course, for Ralph proved too slippery and evasive with his answers. Instead, Mouse began to day-dream about it. He imagined a rambling old farmhouse, with separate stable block for Annie's pony (not that she ever mentioned owning one). Obviously they had servants, but parents were more insubstantial things. Mouse wondered if they were abroad; and when he was in the darkness of the mine he imagined them returning home laden down with rare and wonderful gifts. It helped pass the long minutes before the evening came.

The daily game got under way at about six, but only came into its own at dusk when the light started fading. Then, played out by the glow of candles or the radiance of a woodland fire, it acquired a mystery all its own that made Mouse tremble with anticipation. They played murder in the dark, stalked mythical creatures, fought wars, built camps, dammed streams, and feasted. Sometimes a game demanded they dress up or blacken their faces; while lulls in frantic activity were spent lazing around a camp fire talking. Yet, whatever they did, Ralph, like a beaming ringmaster, was at the centre of all things, making them happen.

Once he organized a treasure hunt in Jerusalem Wood with clues scattered throughout its length. It was a madcap affair with Annie, Clyde, and Mouse streaming through the trees, whooping at the tops of their voices whenever their torches revealed something. The treasure was real. A silver goblet. At the close Mouse drew back, letting Annie find it first, which she did by plunging her hand into the hollow of a tree. Then it was hers. Ralph said he'd have her name engraved upon it.

But always, at the end of each evening, the Pendreds departed. From his window Mouse watched as the Land Rover's tail lights disappeared from sight and hated it. It was like being left behind. Around him he felt the shell of the house breathing out its emptiness from every damp room, the darkness thickening at the windows. But there was also another reason why Mouse hated the night.

The truth finally came out after Ralph made a joking reference to the number of night-lights Mouse was using. He said, 'You must be burning them all night, Mouse'; and Mouse blurted out what he feared.

'A ghost!' uttered Clyde, sitting bolt upright on Mouse's bed.

'I don't believe such stuff,' said Annie. 'I bet you need the candles because you're afraid of the dark.'

Mouse glared at her. This was precisely the reason he had never mentioned it before.

'Hold on, Annie,' said Ralph, leaning against the mantel. 'Let's hear what Mouse has to say first.'

Mouse was embarrassed and defensive, pausing as he spoke as if ready to be interrupted or, in Annie's case, ridiculed.

'I've not seen nothin' . . . But I hear it . . . It's a kinda, kinda noise in the walls . . . a scratching sound, then something bumping—'

'Must be mice,' said Clyde immediately losing interest.

Mouse shook his head. 'No, sometimes I hear a voice, too—but I can't make out what it says . . . and I . . . I keep remembering that the lake was filled in because someone from the house died there . . . '

'And you think it's his ghost?' said Clyde.

Mouse shrugged. 'Dunno . . . sometimes. But I tell you something.' He looked at Annie. 'I'm not scared. I'm used to big places and the dark and being left on m'own. So nobody can say that.'

'Of course not, sunshine,' said Ralph. 'Nobody believes such a thing. Truly. But this is intriguing news, Mouse. It needs investigating.'

Clyde bounced up and down on the bed until its springs wheezed. 'A ghost hunt you mean, Ralph? Are we going to have a ghost hunt? When, Ralph? When?'

'Why not tonight?' said Ralph. 'We'll track down Mouse's ghost and force it to tell us how it met its grisly end.' He grinned so Mouse was unsure if he was amused or excited at the prospect. He said, 'Do you hear the voice every night, Mouse?'

Mouse nodded. 'After you go home.'

'How convenient,' said Annie, pulling a face. 'Anyway, Ralph, how will we manage to stay out all night, don't forget Ma—'

'Leave it to me, Annie old thing,' said Ralph quickly interrupting her. 'We'll ask to go camping then act as if we were, by packing the tents and things.' He smiled at Mouse as if thanking him for making it possible. 'What could be easier?' he said.

Mouse felt ill at ease for the remainder of the day. What if nothing happened? He couldn't stand to disappoint Ralph; then Annie started using sarcasm against him. Coming through the wood, a twig snapped and she said, 'Must be the ghost.'

Back at the house, Ralph carried a big hamper of food upstairs for a picnic and the four of them crowded on to Mouse's bed as if it were a raft out at sea. Along with the hamper came Ralph's idea to fill the room with lots of candles. 'Atmosphere,' he said, but soon it grew unbearably hot. Clyde was another irritation, so excited was he and ready to be scared by anything or nothing at all. As a result he talked too much, and most of what he said was nonsense.

The food went quickly and the empty hours stretched before them. They played cards, one game running into another, until even Mouse was yawning. It was then that they heard the noise.

'What is it, Ralph?' breathed Annie, and Mouse was gratified to see her startled expression.

'Shh!' Ralph jumped up and pressed an ear to the wall. 'Let's go down to the next floor,' he said.

'But—'

'Trust me.'

Candles in hand they edged out on to the shadowy top landing. No longer could they hear anything, but it hardly mattered any more, for imagination had taken its hold. Suddenly Clyde gave a shout. He had seen something— he was sure he had . . . On closer inspection it turned out to be nothing more dangerous or frightening than a discarded newspaper.

'I thought it was alive,' he protested.

'Oh, just be quiet, stupid,' snapped Annie.

Then down the stairs and into a small, dark room at the twist of the landing, considered by all to be Clyde's domain since here, in various hutches and cages along one wall, he housed his menagerie of guinea pigs and chinchillas. The noise obviously unsettled the creatures, who scratched nervously amongst the straw, their eyes glinting like glass in the candlelight.

Bump—bump—scrape . . .

The noise, still muffled, was louder than before.

Clyde pointed his finger. 'It's c-coming from that cupboard,' he said.

Ralph immediately strode up to it—unable to do so quietly in his stout leather shoes— and yanked the doors apart.

After a long, tense silence Mouse whispered, 'What is it, Ralph? What do you see?'

'Nothing,' muttered Ralph darkly.

'L-let's go—pl-please, Ralph,' begged Clyde, close to tears. 'I-I'm scared.'

'Shhh! It'll be all right, I tell you.'

Bump—scrape—bump—scrape . . .

By candlelight Ralph examined the cupboard more closely. He climbed inside it, so they could no longer see him, only hear his breathing.

'What d'ya know?' he called at length.

'What is it?' asked Annie.

'A secret door—I think . . . Damn! I can't get it to budge . . . The shelves are screwed to it.'

By this time Mouse, Annie, and Clyde were pressing so tightly around the cupboard that their faces were practically touching.

'Can you make out what's on the other side?' asked Mouse impatiently.

'No, but I'll find out soon enough,' said Ralph. And from his pocket they saw him take out his penknife.

Quickly the first six screws came out and down came the top shelf. Ralph bundled it to Annie.

'Ralph,' she said biting her bottom lip, 'I'm not sure we should be doing this.'

But Ralph was unstoppable. He couldn't remove the remaining shelves swiftly enough, spurred on by the mysterious scraping and bumping sounds that came in short bursts and were clearly heard above the squeak of loosening screws. Down came the second shelf. The third soon after. Then frustration. The screws securing the lowest shelf had rusted. Ralph muttered under his breath—and when the penknife slipped, scoring the wood and grazing his knuckles, he cursed aloud.

With effort he managed to extract all but one screw which was so badly rusted it refused to turn. Slowly Ralph's shoulders hunched, and in a sudden bout of temper he seized the shelf, ripping it out with his bare hands. Wood splintered—rust crumbled—and the secret door swung ajar.

For a good half minute nobody moved. All eyes were fixed to the door—or, more precisely, to the strip of darkness it revealed to them. Then Ralph picked up his candle and gently pushed the door. It glided open without a sound. Behind it was a rough brick wall entirely covered in a translucent skin of cobwebs—and, more intriguing, the first few steps of a staircase descending into a well of darkness.

Urgent glances were exchanged. Faces looked bemused—worried. Then Ralph grinned. He went up to the opening, stooped his head and passed through. It was like the breaking of a spell. Mouse followed with Clyde and Annie treading on his heels.

The descent was very steep, very straight, and very narrow. They went slowly and with care, for the steps were rough and uneven with no two alike. Ralph at the front cleared the way of trailing cobwebs, but others came, drifting out of the darkness into their faces and hair.

Suddenly Clyde sneezed and with such violence that he took everyone—including himself—by surprise. They froze, the sound still ringing in their ears. When it died Ralph made no attempt to go on.

'What's wrong?' Mouse whispered over his shoulder.

'There's a light,' hissed Ralph. 'Something's ahead.' And he snuffed out his candle.

Clumsily they pressed on, feeling their way with their feet and fingers. Presently the light grew strong enough to see by and the stairway opened into a cool, dingy room. They entered it behind some large barrels. On a shelf a candle flickered. Then a familiar voice came muttering through the gloom. 'Damn fine . . . Damn good.'

Peering between the barrels the children saw the shadowy figure of Joe. His grubby dressing gown hung open revealing even grubbier pyjamas, while in his hand he clutched a jam jar of clear liquid. He was grinning crookedly at his cat—toasting Napoleon's health—muttering, 'Damn fine . . . Damn good,' every time he took a swig.

Tipping back his head he quickly drained the jam jar empty and slammed it down. The children spied on him, while Napoleon, prowling along a dusty top shelf, suspiciously eyed the children. Only Joe was unaware of his audience as he merrily went back to work: rolling—half dragging—a wooden barrel across the floor.

Bump—scrape—bump—scrape . . .

They had found Mouse's ghost.

Clyde giggled.

As they watched, the old man moved several more barrels, breaking off to refill his jam jar from one of them and toast Napoleon all over again. Then, apparently satisfied by his work, he lurched from the room, spilling hot wax down his dressing gown as he went. Napoleon left with him, following close on the backs of his down-trodden slippers.

A door was heard to lock and in the darkness Ralph quickly relit his own candle. Everyone burst out laughing.

'But I don't understand!' wailed Clyde. 'What's Joe up to?'

He trotted after the others as they came creeping out from behind the barrels. Scattered about the room were cobwebby bottles and demijohns, cauldrons, meshes, metal funnels, and jars of crystals; while set squarely in the middle of the floor was a crude brick oven.

Clyde looked even more perplexed. 'Is Joe a wizard?' he said.

'Of sorts,' grinned Ralph. He unscrewed a bottle and sniffed at its contents. 'Why, the cunning old devil has his own liquor still. He's been making vodka. No wonder his nose is as red as it is.'

'Isn't that against the law?' asked Annie.

'Totally.'

Suddenly Mouse, who had wandered off into a dark corner, gave a shout. 'Hey, you lot, come over here,' he called. 'This must be the old wine cellar. Look, the racks are still in place—and they're stuffed with bottles.' He blew off the dust and began reading aloud from the faded labels: 'Peapod wine . . . turnip wine . . . elderflower champagne . . . Wow! Some of these are over twenty years old.'

Ralph started a game to see who could find the most unlikely ingredient to have lent itself to Joe's particular talent. But Joe outsmarted them. It seemed he possessed a genius for turning every part of any vegetable, fruit, or flower into an alcoholic beverage of some sort.

'I wondered why he was so keen on gardening,' said Annie. 'I mean, did you ever see Joe touch a fresh vegetable? I think he survives on boiled eggs and toast.'

'Well,' said Mouse, 'old Joe's got more wine here than he could drink in a hundred years.'

'And what's more,' added Ralph with a strange smile on his lips, 'we now know his secret.'

CHAPTER TEN

It was perhaps then Ralph's plan took form in his mind. Later, back in Mouse's room, he sat by the fire thoughtfully gazing into the flames. The others, who knew better than to disturb him, lay whispering upon Mouse's bed.

Next day, Ralph called them together to announce his idea.

'It's plain stupid,' was the way he fired off, pacing up and down on the floor before them. 'We do all the hard work. Digging, getting soaked through—spending hours in that stinking mud—and where does the biggest part of our reward go? I'll tell you where— straight into the seat pocket of Bart's jeans! I blame myself. We should have been dealing directly with the shops ages ago. We should have been advertising—making contact with the serious bottle collector, getting ourselves known. And what's more, we should have been branching out—doing different things.'

He sounded angry, as if suddenly realizing

he had been cheated.

Mouse looked puzzled. 'What d'you mean, Ralph?' he asked.

'What I'm trying to say, sunshine, is why sell empty bottles? Bottles are made for putting things in. So why don't we do just that? I'm going to speak to Joe this morning, get him to trade some of his home-made wine with us. Think of it: a genuine Victorian bottle containing country wine, made from a hundred-year-old recipe—oh well, we can claim that. Who'll know? Tell you what, I'll get some fancy labels printed with flowers and scrolls and old-fashioned writing . . . It's a sure-fire idea. We can't lose.'

Annie lowered her head. She sounded apologetic. 'Are you sure Joe will go along with you, Ralph? You know what a hoarder he is when it comes to food and I—'

Ralph snorted, sweeping her words aside as if they were nothing. 'Leave all that to me, Annie,' he said. 'Don't I always smooth the way, and this isn't the time to go cold on me. It's going to work I tell you, I've thought it through from top to bottom.'

'Yes, Ralph,' she agreed meekly. She lowered her head still further, letting her hair fall across her face.

For the first time Mouse felt angry with Ralph. Everything was turning slightly sour. Whereas once the company spent several mornings a week below ground at the Big Daddy, Ralph now insisted they go every day; and in the mine two new side galleries were opened.

'We have to build up our bottle stocks, old things,' said Ralph chivvying them along.

Within a short while the effect of their extra shifts began to show at the hall. Room after room brimmed and gleamed with empty bottles. They spilled out on to the landings preventing the playing of games—not that they had time for games; Ralph said they had better things to do.

And all the while his grand scheme gathered pace.

One afternoon, Clyde, Annie, and Mouse returned dirty and exhausted from the Big Daddy to find most of Joe's home-made wine brought up from the cellar; and, in one of the remaining empty rooms, trestle tables were set out at intervals, making it resemble a factory production line.

Ralph smiled. 'See, I told you Joe would be a pussycat. In fact, he was pleased to help. I gave him some cigarettes and chocolate and he was over the moon.'

Afternoons thereafter grew to be as dreary as mornings. No longer did they play cards or lounge about listening to the radio. No longer did they sit toasting endless rounds of bread, feeding the crusts to the guinea pigs. Instead they washed bottles—scrubbing them clean—because Ralph said the wine would turn to vinegar if they didn't. And the scrubbed bottles needed filling, corking, labelling, and loading on to the back of the Land Rover.

Soon Mouse grew to hate the sickly sweet smell of wine and the angry wasps it attracted, swarming around the spillages. He hated it, not for his own sake, but for Annie's.

He watched her, her hands plunged into cold water; they were red and like the hands of an old woman. She paused to brush a strand of hair from her face. She looked tired and pale.

'Chop-chop, Annie old thing,' said Ralph cheerily. 'Nearly done.'

Imperceptibly, Ralph had changed too. Often moody, and irritable, he grew quicker at finding fault: this bottle wasn't clean enough, that cork was crooked, they were way behind schedule . . . And usually, by eight o'clock, everyone was so tired that the Pendreds went straight home, leaving Mouse to his own company.

One night, on the pretence of asking for matches, Mouse crept downstairs and tapped at Joe's door.

There was no reply.

The boy tried to remember the last time he

had seen the old man. It was over a week ago. Perhaps something was wrong. Perhaps he was sick.

He opened the door and was relieved to see the lone oil lamp burning steadily against the gloom, throwing up its trail of greasy smoke that marked the walls and ceiling.

'Joe?' he called softly.

Napoleon went prowling along the top of a tall bookcase, his shadow enlarged and menacing upon the wall. He stopped, arched his back and spat.

'Joe?'

A sob broke. 'Go 'vay. Leave me. Vhat more you damn can take?'

The frail voice arose from behind a chair. As Mouse went towards it he noticed something was changed about the shabby room. Suddenly he realized. Joe's ancient stockpile of food had disappeared, and only circles in the dust remained to show where it had lain undisturbed for so many years.

Mouse stood still, looking about him. Despite a clumsy attempt to conceal them, he saw the tins of food at once, behind cushions, under the shapeless sofa, and even covered over by a rug.

'What's the matter, Joe?' asked Mouse, going forward a few more steps. He could see the wispy grey hair of the old man pressed close to the back of the chair. 'What's made you like this?'

'Nazis and Communiztz.' The old man's voice sounded bitter. 'Vhich damn vun are you, boy?'

'I don't know what you're babbling on about, Joe. Honest. I swear I don't.'

Mouse squatted on his heels beside the old man's chair. His tone remained kindly; but the old man was as resentful as a child.

'You take vhat you damn vell vont. I, old man, cannot have power to stop you. You snap me like a damn tvig iv you vish.'

Without protesting he allowed Mouse to help him up in his seat, lifting his head to receive a greasy cushion.

'Now s'pose you tell me what's up?' said the boy. 'What's got into you to make you want to hide your stuff?'

Joe grew agitated again. Foam appeared at the corners of his mouth as he spoke. 'To stop him damn stealing ov me—me, an old man who haz known real hunger in Poland vhen da—'

'Yeah, Joe,' said Mouse impatiently. 'That was then. Who would want to pinch your food now?'

'That damn boy! Him vith da angel smile. But he no angel. I tell you that damn boy iz a devil!'

'Ralph?' said Mouse, smiling with disbelief.

'You mean Ralph?'

'Ya. He da damn thief.'

'Come on, Joe, why on earth would Ralph want to nick your food?'

'You damn azk him!' cried Joe furiously. 'He rob me ov my vine. He zay, you have too much to drink, Joe, let me have some. Noh! He zay okay, I go and tell everyvun Joseph Dabrowski make hiz own vodka. Thiz 'gainzt da law. They put me—an old broken man—'gainzt da vall and bang-bang: vun old man lezz in da vorld.'

Mouse pretended he didn't understand. 'You telling me, Joe, that Ralph is blackmailing you over the vodka into handing over all your home-made wine?'

Joe nodded vigorously. 'And I only drink my *wódka* for medicine reasonz. I damn sick old man—*you* know.'

'Ralph wouldn't do that.' Mouse smiled again, only this time it was with less certainty. '*Would* he?'

'Ya!' snapped Joe. 'He damn vould. He damn doez. I tell you da truth boy . . . Ach! Go learn et for yourself.'

Mouse didn't believe Joe. Not entirely. Yet the story had set an uncertainty at the back of his mind that refused to be quiet. The easiest course would be to ask Ralph straight out.

But, whether it was true or false, Mouse knew that with a few easy words Ralph would win him round and he'd end up apologizing for even considering such a thing in the first place. Then, two days after this, something else happened that left Mouse in no doubt about the way Ralph worked.

Earlier in the morning Ralph had casually announced a meeting with a *business colleague* in one of the better rooms downstairs. He was wearing a dark suit, and with his hair slicked back might have been sixteen. But there was something sinister about him too—the reverse of a dwarf pretending to be a child.

He said, 'I don't want this chap knowing I operate from up at the hall, so you lot best stay hidden. Understand?'

His voice was hard. But as if remembering, he smiled warmly and patted Mouse's shoulder saying, 'Keep up the good work, sunshine.'

About mid morning Ralph's bottle-washers heard the well-oiled purr of an expensive car, its wheels crunching on the gravel.

Curious, they crowded about the window to admire the sleek black Mercedes. But Mouse reacted strangely, suddenly reeling away and pressing his back to the wall.

'What's wrong?' asked Clyde staring at him as if he were mad.

Mouse was unable to speak at first.

'It's him,' he eventually managed to say in a broken voice. 'It's Herod Pinner . . .'

CHAPTER ELEVEN

'I can't see what your problem is, Mouse,' said Ralph airily, as he drove the Land Rover to the Big Daddy. 'Truly I can't.' The Land Rover's windows were open, filling the cab with the sound of its engine and the smell of dry earth. 'Whenever Mr Pinner comes, you just keep your head low and out of sight. What could be simpler?'

Mouse was shocked. 'He's coming *again*?'

'Of course,' said Ralph, as if it were the most natural thing in the world. 'He likes my ideas and he's a man with contacts. As much as I hate to admit it, sunshine, we need your Mr Pinner. For a start, it's against the law for us kids to deal in alcohol—besides, he thinks we could move on to bigger and better things, and is willing to finance us. We would be stupid not to use his experience. He told me we should be gearing up for Christmas.'

'Christmas is months away yet,' said Annie.

'With lots of hard work to be done in the meantime,' observed Ralph.

Clyde raised his sun-glasses. 'Will he make us lots of money, Ralph?'

'Horrible gleaming heaps,' grinned Ralph.

'But you don't understand,' protested Mouse. 'Pinner is bad. Bad and dangerous. I know what he's like and what he can do. Please, Ralph, don't have anything more to do with him. He'll only—'

'Tell you what, sunshine,' said Ralph staring straight ahead. 'I'll buy you something nice. A present. Something to cheer you up. How about that?'

Later on, Annie touched Mouse's arm. 'It'll be all right, Mouse,' she promised. 'Nobody'll hurt you.'

Mouse wasn't so sure.

From then on, the black Mercedes appeared often before Coldby Hall; and *there* was Pinner in his baggy suit and brash silk tie. Such intense interest in the house and bottle business was peculiar considering his many other commitments. Ralph took to wearing a pink carnation in his button-hole. He seemed to swell, grow larger than life. Mouse, on the other hand, lived on an edge, constantly listening for the approach of a car. The crunch of tyres on the gravel drive his signal to slip out of the back door and seek refuge up at Jerusalem Wood, running all the way.

The Pendreds hadn't a hope of understanding the fear Mouse felt at such times. It was fear that kept the boy skulking at the wood for hours on end—sometimes until it had grown dark. Ralph said nothing, but was clearly annoyed. To him Mouse was silly, over-reacting—and worst of all—time-wasting.

Mouse grew deeply unhappy.

'Why is Ralph doing this?' he angrily blurted out to Annie. 'He'll be sorry. You see.' He shook his head and muttered, 'We'll all be sorry.'

Annie shrugged. Pinner was again at the hall and she and Mouse had climbed a tree overlooking the lake-site.

'Suppose Ralph thinks it's for the best,' she said. She was too hot to argue. The afternoon was close and sticky and she fanned herself with a leaf. 'You have to learn to trust Ralph,' she continued. 'Can't you just forget about the time you worked for Pinner. I mean, you managed to forget everything else.'

'That's different,' protested Mouse. 'Don't you think I want to remember all that stuff before the car crash—about having a mum and dad and everything? . . . You're lucky. You've got a proper home.' And Mouse couldn't resist adding, 'Although you wouldn't think so because no one ever says a single word about it.'

Annie pulled a face. 'That's Ralph. He likes it best that way. Clyde and me, well . . . we go along with him. But I'll tell you something, Mouse.' She lowered her voice. 'And don't you dare let on to Ralph I told you so, but . . . we aren't the way you like to think us. You want us to be all wonderful and perfect but it's not—'

'Hey, you two!'

The urgent shout came from below. Looking down, they saw Clyde impatiently staring up at them, his face red with excitement.

'What do you want, pest?' asked Annie.

'Okay, I won't tell you then.'

'What?'

'There's two strange men in the woods,' blurted out Clyde, who never could keep a secret.

At that same moment Mouse and Annie heard the distant rumble of motor bikes, and Mouse knew at once who it was.

'Vinnie,' he said.

Within seconds, Vinnie and Jinks had burst free of the woodland and were scudding across the hummocks. Neither wore a crash helmet and Jinks's greasy hair flew out in strips. Turning, they raced along the flat edge of the clearing, front wheels high in the air, jealously lashing out at each other as they came alongside. As constant as the engines' straining whine was Jinks's idiotic laughter.

'See!' cried Mouse watching them in utter dismay. 'I knew this would happen. I knew it!'

'Come on, Mouse,' said Annie impatiently. 'We've got to get down from here. Quick! Before we're spotted.'

At the foot of the tree Clyde was bursting to tell more of his news.

'They've got a crossbow,' he announced at once. 'And been shooting at starlings and pigeons . . . and . . . and everything. See the big one? Well, he fancies himself as a bit of a poacher. And they've come into the woods looking for deer. I know because I heard him tell the other one.'

'Huh, typical of Vin,' said Mouse bitterly. 'He was always cruel to things smaller than himself.'

Just then the engines revved loudly before dying back into silence. Swigging down the last drop of his Special Brew, Vinnie threw the can to the ground and shot it at close range with the crossbow. Like a living thing, the punctured can leapt twisting into the air. Jinks watched and snorted leerily through his nose.

'Giss a go, Vin,' he pleaded. 'You said.'

Slyly, Vinnie took the dog-end cigarette

from his mouth and with a vicious jab stubbed it on the back of Jinks's hand. Jinks yelped and cursed.

'Why you do that, Vin?' he said, sulkily nursing the hand to his chest.

Vinnie grinned. ''Cos, my son, you're getting too lippy for m'liking.'

So saying, he high-kicked his leg over the saddle and stood with the cigarette butt gripped between his teeth and the crossbow held high on his shoulder, self-consciously arrogant. Narrowing his eyes he scanned the clearing. The only dumb animal worth shooting was Jinks. The thought put the grin back on his face.

Deprived of real game, he idled away the minutes by aiming at birds and insects. Then he fired a shot at random. It crashed into the undergrowth close to Clyde, convincing Annie they shouldn't stay a moment longer.

'Where can we go?' protested Mouse. 'There's nowhere else left.'

This was true, but neither could they stay. As they rose to leave, Vinnie's eye caught the movement. He hooted triumphantly, at the same time loosing another bolt. With tremendous force it thudded into a trunk, embedding itself there.

'Missed,' sneered Jinks, unimpressed.

Vinnie regarded him coldly. Throwing aside

his cigarette, he lurched forward with that peculiar high-stepping gait of his.

'There's one there, Jinksy me ol' son,' he insisted. 'A big 'un.'

But Jinks moodily went on getting his fingers oily amongst the workings of his engine, pretending not to hear.

Reaching the edge of the clearing and finding nothing, Vinnie lost interest, too. He turned to walk away, but before he did he fired a last, malicious shot into the trees, and Mouse felt a terrible searing pain in his arm.

'Mouse!' gasped Annie as he stumbled and fell.

Framed by the main doorway of the hall, Ralph stood watching.

Unaware that anything was wrong he scuttled down the garden steps and said angrily, 'Where have you been? I've been waiting here for hours.'

Annie glared at him.

He turned uncomprehendingly to Mouse whose good arm was wrapped around Annie's shoulder. The boy's face was grey. Shock most likely, for the actual wound was only flesh deep. Mouse stumbled into him.

'Hey, watch it, pal!' he squawked. 'God, you've mucked up my suit now.'

Blood dotted the hallway tiles: vivid red on

the grimy white and black. In his room it dripped steadily into the sink as the Pendreds roughly tugged Mouse's jumper and shirt over his head.

Everyone was talking at once.

'I think I might throw up,' droned Mouse over and over again.

'Do you think he'll die?' prattled Clyde. 'He might you know—he might . . .'

'Ralph, he needs a doctor,' said Annie. 'We need to fetch a doctor . . .'

Suddenly Ralph pressed his hands to his ears, letting his anger explode from him with a terrific shout. 'Give me space to think, will you! I'm sick of it! Why does everyone have to rely on me for everything—at every minute of the day?'

In the shocked silence Ralph smiled weakly and tried to shrug off his outburst. 'Listen, old things,' he said more calmly. 'It's not as bad as it seems. Look, go rip up a sheet for bandages will you. I'll see to Mouse here. Good old Mouse. You'll be fine, old fellow. Truly.'

The bleeding stopped soon after, but Mouse remained in a state of shock. He lay on his bed trembling uncontrollably. By his side he heard a bottle being uncorked, then a pungent smell hit his senses.

'Get this down you, sunshine,' said Ralph

encouragingly. 'It's Joe's *medicine*. You'll feel much better after some of this.'

Before Mouse could object the hard mouth of a bottle met his own, filling it with a burning, tasteless liquid. He gagged as it hit his throat, the fire racing through his body. He tried to struggle, but Ralph roughly held him down, tipping the bottle higher. Unable to draw breath, Mouse felt he was drowning in vodka.

With a final swipe of his hand he knocked the bottle aside and staggered from the room. How strange . . . No longer could he judge the distance of the floor. He pulled himself up, just short of plunging into the stairwell. From somewhere Ralph was calling, but Mouse's head was swimming. He didn't understand the meaning of words any more; and around him familiar objects conspired to look different—so dark and threatening.

Bursting through a door he saw what he thought was a pool of water to cool his burning body. And yet, when he waded into it, the water was glass—ranks of blue poison bottles, glowing softly in the half light. They went down with a terrific clatter, skittling in all directions. Mouse glanced about him, beyond understanding any of it.

He decided to remain where he was and groped blindly for the floor-boards, lurching into the chaos of scattering bottles. But now the room itself was beginning to tip and spin as if the house had sprouted wings and was flying through the air.

Spinning . . .

Spinning . . .

Faster and faster.

Then everything slid away into darkness.

CHAPTER TWELVE

'Ever so, ever so sorry, Mouse,' said Ralph contritely. 'Truly I am.'

He said this every time he visited Mouse's bedside; and with every visit came an expensive present. (The wristwatch alone must have cost a fortune.) After two days, when Mouse felt well enough to eat again, Ralph turned up clutching a huge basket of fruit and danced round the room with the pineapple on his head. Mouse thrived on all the attention he received. He almost enjoyed being an invalid because he could pretend things had returned to how they used to be.

But a week later it was September and the new school term began.

It was next to impossible imagining any of the three Pendreds confined to a classroom—especially Ralph. As for Mouse, school held no terrors—he washed bottles instead; and for company he visited Joe.

At first the old man regarded Mouse with deep suspicion. But since Mouse never called empty-handed—bringing with him biscuits and even the tea, sugar, and milk to brew up with—the old man came first to accept, then to expect these visits, leaving the door slightly open in anticipation of them.

Then, one afternoon, as Mouse was setting out the two chipped mugs, Joe gripped his wrist—his touch was hot and dry—and gently he pushed Mouse's hand aside. With a great air of mystery the old man then produced a tea caddy and nudged it towards the boy, indicating that he should take from that instead. The tea, when brewed, was awful, the leaves must have been years old. Without complaint Mouse forced it down, every last drop. That he did so was an act of kindness to show how much he appreciated the old man's gesture.

'You no have parentz, boy?' Joe enquired as he poured a generous tot of vodka into his mug. 'No *matka*—no *ojciec*?'

'Both dead, Joe.'

'In da var?'

'No—car crash. Because of it I can't remember anything about them or, for that matter, anything about myself up to the time it happened.'

'Vhatz thiz you say—you have no past?'

Mouse shook his head.

'Mine in here, boy,' said Joe, tapping the side of his head. 'Et com' to me every night. I remember every lazt and liddle detail.'

Mouse said, 'Who's luckiest, I wonder?'

As Joe grew to trust Mouse more, he revealed to him little fragments of his own life. He had pitifully few personal things, and none of any worth, but his most treasured possession was a heavy leather album of yellowing photographs, all adrift between the tissue sheets.

'You look,' he said bluntly.

Mouse went slowly through it, feeling the old man's sadness like a dull ache.

Joseph Dabrowski, pictured as a handsome young officer in the Polish army, grinning at the camera beside his Wikov sports car, a cigarette smoking rakishly in his hand . . . on leave, strolling down a main street in Warsaw, arm in arm with pretty women and fellow officers . . . attending a wedding, the guests all correct and solemn . . .

Joe remembered the names of every one there. Most were dead. 'Turn over . . . turn over,' he pleaded when it grew too much and he held a filthy handkerchief to his streaming eyes.

Another page and more memories: a forgotten summer on a lake, the women beneath parasols, the men all in white . . . the family's country house, with the estate workers and servants thronging the steps, looking quaint and afraid, as if they had never been photographed before and seeming to distrust the entire business.

Next, deep in dust from the top of a wardrobe, came a shoe box containing medals and buttons and cigarette cards. Rummaging through the bundles of letters and broken oddments, Mouse came upon things that were curiously moving, like the curl of hair in a locket, and the key to a door that no longer existed. Worthless to others, but priceless in Joe's eyes. Lovingly he packed everything back into place and hid the box away again.

'Gone,' he murmured. 'All gone. Damn Nazis and Communiztz take everything and da people zo hungry they eat da poor damn animalz in da zoo.'

Then one day Joe began talking in a slow, trembling voice. Only after a while did Mouse realize he was telling him the story of his life . . .

His family, the Dabrowskis, were once rich land-owners. They had an estate in the country, town house in Warsaw, and a cottage by the Baltic Sea. These apart, they also owned a paper mill and bottling factory.

Life was easy and comfortable for the

Dabrowskis, cushioned as they were from the outside world. Then war broke out and they quickly discovered it was no longer a question of being rich or poor: it was merely enough to be Polish to have so many enemies and be utterly despised. Its borders swiftly overrun, Poland was divided and shared by its two aggressive neighbours—Nazi Germany in the west and Communist Russia in the east. From that moment on, the Communists and Nazis moved to destroy the Polish nation for ever.

Naturally, the Polish people resisted as best they could, but the odds were hopelessly stacked against them. The German army alone possessed nearly three thousand tanks, the Poles had less than two hundred. Joe, a cavalry officer, rode with his regiment. They resembled toy soldiers going to war, mounted and with swords drawn, riding to face machine guns. In a matter of seconds a hundred of them were mowed down, with Joe one of the first to fall, his horse shot from beneath him.

Later, coming to, he found himself face down in the mud, where he had been left for dead. Stealing civilian clothes and living by his wits, he trekked across open country to the family estate. The house was looted and in darkness. Every member of his family had been taken away and were probably dead already. But amidst the broken glass lay a foreign postcard from his younger sister, Bronia. It had arrived the day before the invasion. At least he knew for sure one member of his family was safe.

Tucking the postcard into his pocket, he made his way to Warsaw.

The city—including the Dabrowski town house—was a burnt-out ruin. Joe managed to lay hands on forged identity documents and existed the sort of half life everyone led at the time. His greatest mistake, however, was in thinking life would be more bearable in the eastern sector under the Russians. He escaped from Warsaw and five days later, on Christmas Eve 1939, was arrested.

Ironically, it was Bronia's postcard, which Joe had kept as a token of luck and hope, that proved his downfall. The Russian soldiers who searched him—big raw-faced peasants in ill-fitting boots—could barely read a single word of their own language, still less of Polish. They arrested Joe for, of all things, being in possession of a foreign stamp.

'I remember that damn stamp—that *znaczek*—az iv et waz before me thiz moment,' said Joe. 'Et yellow and on et waz a damn elephant. Ha! for thiz they accuze me ov plotting vith enemiez overseaz and give to me ten damn yearz hard labour.'

He passed through a series of prisons, from Drohobycz to Lwow, from Lwow to Odessa, the cells growing increasingly more squalid and crowded. One bitterly cold day in February he was herded on to a cattle truck, already crammed to bursting with fellow Poles, for the nightmare journey to Vladivostock. So tightly were they packed there was no room to lie down, there was no stove and occasionally a few crusts or salted herrings were tossed in to be fought over. In Joe's truck ten died. He had lice, a hacking cough, and sores covering him from head to foot.

Nor was the nightmare over when the train finally halted. Barely human any more, the prisoners were loaded into the airless, black hold of a ship and carried across the sea of Japan to Magadan, then up the Kolyma river to the gold mines of Maldiak. Of course, many more died on the way, of cold or fever, or for the simple reason they gave up the will to live; those who survived envied them the luxury of death.

Against the blistering cold the prisoners wrapped themselves in rags which in time thickened with filth; and any piece of sacking, no matter how coarse, was seized upon for its capacity to lend extra warmth. They were literally sealed into their clothing and the only way to undress was to cut themselves free. At night they slept in huts roofed only in canvas, one hundred prisoners to each hut, all curled up and shivering on bare log bunks. At five o'clock a guard bellowed at them to get up.

'Stop stinking in your pit, you no good lazy Poles!' he shouted. 'What's the use you dreaming of sausages and vodka?' This was his grim little joke each morning.

After some dry bread and gruel, the lines trickled away to the mines in the forest. Another piece of dark humour was the orchestra that stood playing in the snow as the prisoners trudged by.

The ground was frozen so hard they needed chisels to crack it, and the gruelling, back-breaking work went on until eight o'clock at night, unless the guards decided they hadn't worked hard enough, in which case an extra two hours were added to their labour.

For eight months Joe endured this and many other cruelties; but knowing he wasn't strong enough to last another winter he seized upon a desperate scheme to escape. Five times he threw himself off a log, until finally he succeeded in breaking his own arm. He knew from experience that if the camp's hospital was full he would be sent back to work with his arm untreated. It was a risk he was willing to take.

However, luck was with him. He was transferred back west, working as a welder until 1941, when the Russians announced an amnesty for Polish prisoners. Once freed he escaped to Turkey and from Turkey made his way to Britain.

There the war ended for him. When he attempted to enlist the doctors pronounced him unfit (one calling him a living skeleton). But at least in England he was reunited with Bronia. She had married an English pilot—the then master of Coldby Hall—who was killed in action two years later.

After the war, with nothing in Poland to go back to, Joe and Bronia settled down together until Bronia's death twelve years ago.

Wearily Joe shook his head. 'I dream every night ov theze thingz,' he whispered. 'I see every face. Every vun. I relive my life again.'

And Mouse, who had no real past to dream about, dreamt of Joe's past. And Mouse was always the shuffling prisoner, and Ralph always the smiling guard. And the mine was like a human mouth; and what sparkled through the darkness was not gold but glass. Bottle glass.

CHAPTER THIRTEEN

'No Ralph today?' called Mouse, buttoning up his coat as he came out of the hall and down the steps.

Annie and Clyde stood waiting for him, heavily muffled against a hoary November frost. Clyde's face was completely hidden inside his hood, and their breath hung white in the air.

Neither bothered making the effort to reply. Ralph was so busy these days with one thing or another that he rarely went with them to the mine. If he showed up at all it would be much later on, and then he'd be dressed in his suit so unable to go underground.

With Clyde yawning and Annie stamping her feet, they shuffled across to the Land Rover, hidden at the side of the house.

Mouse had been driving for about a month now. He was not yet as good as Ralph, but improving all the time. He parked up in the woods, beneath trees stark and lifeless—ready for winter.

At the mine, Annie quickly lit the charcoal in an old oil drum and they silently gathered around it sharing the warmth. Frost lingered in the air, forming long vaporous trails. Underfoot the ground was solid. When Mouse entered the mine, ice cracked beneath his knees, and even deep below ground, the cold made the clay stubborn and unwilling to yield its possessions.

The boy worked until his fingers were numb and water had seeped into his waterproof clothing. Back in daylight once more he blinked at the ice-bright sky.

Still no sign of Ralph.

Clyde made ready to go next. Annie assuming the role of mother, turned back the cuffs and leggings of his plastic jacket and trousers, which were far too big for him. She needlessly fussed over buttons and gloves. Then he crawled into the dark hole and was gone.

Annie sighed thoughtfully and handed Mouse some soup in a metal cup.

'You know what, Mouse?' she said. 'What I long for more than anything in the world?' She paused. The boy stared at her intently. She said, 'It's for some really bad weather. Endless rain—or better still, snow. Lots and lots of lovely deep snow.'

'Oh, why's that?' said Mouse, although he half guessed.

She said simply, 'Then we won't have to come here,' and hid her face behind her hair as if ashamed at admitting such a thing.

For some reason, perhaps loyalty to Ralph, Mouse began to protest—that it wasn't so bad, that it was bound to get better, that they should remember the good things the mine had given them—when suddenly they heard a crack and a half swallowed boom from deep in the earth, and the ground gave a violent lurch.

As if his fingers had lost their strength, Mouse let the mug of soup drop. Jerking back his head he watched in disbelief as mud, rippling and furrowed like water, came rolling down over the mine's entrance, triggering off yet more slides and falls.

'Clyde!' he heard Annie utter. Then she began to scream.

In a panic they flew at the landslip. It had hardly stopped moving before they were clawing at it with their bare hands. Yet for every armful they scooped clear, three more slithered down to take its place. After ten minutes they had made no headway.

'It's useless!' cried Mouse, dragging Annie away. 'We have to get Ralph!'

'You go, then!' screamed Annie angrily.

'I'm not leaving Clyde.'

'What good will you be here?' shouted Mouse. 'Eh? You'll only bring down more mud and make it worse. We need Ralph. Ralph'll know what to do.' Nervously he ran the back of his hand across his mouth. 'God, Annie,' he said more calmly. 'Please. You've got to come with me and show me the way.'

Annie was sobbing uncontrollably by the time they reached the Land Rover. Even then she refused to get in—refused to desert Clyde. She ran backwards and forwards wringing her hands.

'Annie, get in!' said Mouse sharply. 'You're wasting time!'

And meekly she clambered in beside him, and Mouse started up the engine and roared away at high speed through the woodland.

He drove as a madman might drive—head down like a sprinter, squinting over the steering wheel. Every bump and jolt jarred the vehicle. Flocks of sheep broke and scattered before it, the horn blaring like an angry shout; and at gates he braked so hard that the grass was gouged into ribbons of mud.

Finally they burst out on to the road, the vehicle lurching from one side to the other—clipping the verge, throwing passenger and driver together as they mounted it—then bumping back down on to tarmac again.

Other cars skidded to a halt, all hooting wildly.

Annie, who had ceased sobbing and was unnaturally composed, gave quiet directions. Soon the first straggling buildings of Easton appeared, promising a dull village, which it was, a village bloated by shoe factories and second-hand car lots. Mouse screeched round a corner into a road of grey council houses.

'Stop!' cried Annie.

'Here?' Mouse stared at her.

Despite the desperate race against the clock, Mouse couldn't disguise his amazement. He took a long, slow look, seeing an untended garden bounded by a broken fence and a house as far removed from the one he imagined the Pendreds living in as possible. Upstairs, cheap yellow curtains were drawn against the day; downstairs the gloom of the living-room was occasionally enlivened by a flickering television, revealing an interior that was dreary and cluttered.

At once the front door flew open and Ralph took two strides out. He stood glaring at Mouse. Anger soon followed. He ran to the gate. Dressed in jeans and an old T-shirt he looked closer to his real age and, well, so un-Ralph-like, that Mouse could have passed him in the street and not recognized him.

'What you doing here, Mouse?' he growled.

Even his accent sounded different—less affected.

'Big Daddy . . . ' said Mouse, managing to gasp out the words. 'Clyde's trapped in a mud fall.'

'But you should never have come here,' said Ralph darkly. 'Never-ever.'

Just then a dumpy little woman in an apron trotted down the side of the house. She resembled Annie and was obviously their mother. Noticing Ralph by the Land Rover she looked puzzled.

'Anything the matter, Ralphie?' she called.

Suddenly Ralph leapt in behind Mouse. 'Drive on!' he ordered.

The woman scuttled to the gate to watch the Land Rover disappear down the road. 'Ralphie! Ralphie!' she called after it.

The return journey to the Big Daddy was a tense one. Mouse spent the time trying to recall every last detail before he and Annie fled. Would it be further changed when they returned? Trees uprooted, boulders strewn, cracks opened in the earth? His thoughts ran restlessly along the same lines, and it was as if he could see through Clyde's eyes. He imagined the cold, silent darkness pressing down on him: the Big Daddy locked shut like a clenched jaw.

Nobody spoke inside the cab and Mouse

sensed Ralph's simmering resentment.

Suddenly he blared the horn. Stupid, stupid sheep. They had strayed through an open gate. One *he* had left open. Now the lane was blocked and the Land Rover quickly surrounded. The sheep's fleeces were dirty and matted; their blank moon-struck faces unsettling. Every time Mouse jabbed the horn the sheep bolted in terror, entangling themselves in the hedgerow—running wild as the Land Rover tried to nose its way through.

'Is it necessary to make so much noise?' said Ralph sourly.

Ignoring him, Mouse kept his hand firmly down on the horn until the Land Rover was off the road and racing across deserted fields. The speedometer registered thirty miles an hour . . . forty miles an hour . . . fifty miles an hour; and the vehicle bucked at every dip and hollow as if trying to unseat its passengers.

'Steady . . . steady,' breathed Ralph.

From the top of the last steep incline, Jerusalem Wood spread itself dark in the distance. The Land Rover, in a low whining gear, bounced across a patchwork of fields, at last entering the tangled mass of trees.

The moment they stopped, Ralph snatched the big shovel from the back, threw it over his shoulder and strode off to the mine. Annie and Mouse ran after him.

'Give me space,' said Ralph, digging at the churned earth, only to find, as Annie and Mouse had done, that whatever was excavated was replaced a moment later by a new fall. Unlike them, however, he paused a moment to consider what needed to be done.

'What is it, Ralph?' asked Annie, watching him anxiously.

'We need something to keep the mud back,' he said. 'Quick, you and Mouse fetch plenty of branches, the thicker the better. I want you to push them deep into the ground just over the mine. That should hold it for long enough.'

Annie and Mouse worked tirelessly, dashing backwards and forwards between the wood and Big Daddy.

By creating a fence to hold back the loose earth, the branches did the trick. Yet once the ground gave such an ominous rumble that all three children leapt aside, shouting at each other to stay clear. In the event a mere trickle of stones rattled down and Ralph, stepping up, continued to dig.

Deeper and deeper he went into the earth, the soil soft and musty. And, as ill-dressed as he was for the biting cold, soon his clothes hung wet against his perspiring body; and every part of him was spattered with mud. He was grim and silent, his mind set to the task;

while Mouse and Annie, their offers of help rejected, stood watching and fretting at a distance.

'Look! . . . Look!'

Suddenly Annie was screaming madly.

She pointed and with his hands Ralph cleared the spot, uncovering two pitifully small shoes.

Annie dropped to her knees, alongside her brother, urgently clawing at the soft mud. When the backs of Clyde's legs appeared, the boys roughly dragged the rest of him free, causing another mud-slide that buried the mine for good.

'Is he all right? Is he all right?' Annie was beside herself with worry. She vigorously rubbed the small boy's hand which was icy cold.

Clyde moved. His eyelids flickered. He might have been a small hibernating creature unearthed from its winter's nest. Then, weakly, his voice came floating up.

'I . . . I thought you weren't ever coming,' he said accusingly. 'I couldn't move my legs, and I thought you had left me. And every time I tried to move, more of the roof fell on me, so I lay in the dark and it got colder and colder, and I waited and w-waited. And I tried singing to pass the time, but I had forgotten all the words. And it seemed like a long time.

And I thought you'd left me and weren't ever coming back . . . O-Oh, Annie—' and Clyde began crying as loudly as his sister.

Only Ralph was unmoved. He stumbled across the site of the Big Daddy deep in thought.

Annie shouted to him, her voice thick with emotion: 'Ralph—Clyde's not badly hurt—nothing's broken, I mean.'

'Glad to hear it, old thing,' he replied absently, his easy confidence returned. 'Knew it was not as bad as you made out. Never is. Give him a rest and something to eat and we can all make a fresh start together this afternoon.'

'A fresh start?'

'A new mine,' said Ralph. 'We need to begin straight away before the ground gets really hard.'

'I don't care about that!' cried Annie, suddenly furious. 'Clyde might have been killed today and all you can think of is your precious mine. I tell you I'm fed up with this, Ralph. I'm fed up with everything. I warned you the Big Daddy was dangerous. And we never have any fun any more. Sometimes you act as if we're your servants.'

Ralph burst out laughing, but seeing Annie was deadly serious, he nodded and said, 'Well, yes . . . you're probably right. In fact, I know you are . . . Next year, Annie, we can do so much more together. And I've been thinking . . . well, old thing . . . I haven't bought you anything nice for ages. I must buy you a present—something that'll cheer you up.'

'Don't want anything,' she said, flicking back her hair.

Ralph's expression hardened. Outwardly he remained smiling, but there was no warmth in it.

'I won't give up now,' he said darkly. 'Not for you or anyone else. Just you remember that, Annie.'

'*You* do what *you* want,' she replied haughtily. 'But I'm sick of the cold and mud. I'm sick of dropping into bed every night dog tired and dreaming of nothing but bottles. *Your* stupid bottles, Ralph—'

She yelped as Ralph seized her arm and shook her. 'You'll do it!' he said savagely. 'You'll do it because I tell you to.'

Mouse immediately sprang to her defence. 'Pack it in, Ralph! Leave her alone!'

To his amazement Ralph obeyed. He shoved Annie away from him, letting her stumble and fall in the mud.

'She's right,' Mouse went on. 'It's just like slaving for Pinner. You push us too hard, Ralph.'

Ralph pointed at him with a finger that

trembled with rage. 'Best you keep your nose out of this, pal,' he said. 'You're nothing—a dirty little beggar I once let tag along with us.'

'I've paid you back for whatever I owe,' said Mouse unabashed. 'I've paid you back ten times over. Now I've had it. Mouldy old bottles aren't worth getting killed for.' And before he could stop himself he said, 'I say we go on strike!'

'Me too,' said Annie at once.

Clyde looked fearfully at Ralph. 'And me,' he said at last.

Ralph's resentment fastened on Mouse. '*You* did this,' he said menacingly. '*You* turned my family against me. I'll fix you, pal. I'll fix you for good.'

He turned, kicked over the oil-drum fire and stormed into the wood. They heard the Land Rover start up and roar away into the distance.

'He'll get over it,' said Annie softly.

Mouse stood gazing after his friend, feeling he had done something inexcusably cruel.

Ralph didn't come to the hall the next day, nor the day after that, although Annie and Clyde paid a call, lounging across Mouse's bed in their school uniforms, both full of chatter and bustle; and both acting as if nothing had changed.

'No use you worrying about it,' said Annie good-naturedly. 'Ralph'll come round when he's good and ready.'

'Always was a big sulker,' added Clyde, eating the last of the chocolate biscuits.

But Mouse remained uneasy.

It was shortly before midnight on the third day that he heard someone on the stairs. His tread was too heavy for either Annie or Clyde; and Joe never left the ground floor for fear of bombers. It was Ralph, thought Mouse. Who else could it be but Ralph in his stout leather brogues? And he grinned stupidly with happiness.

He was at the door in a second. Peering around it, he could make nothing out in the blackness of the stairway. It pulled him up like cold water.

'Ralph?'

The feet stopped a moment then again began to climb. Slowly. Step by step nearer to the room at the top.

'That you, Ralph?'

Only the sinister tip-tap of feet upon bare boards answered.

Was this one of Ralph's games? Perhaps that's why he didn't answer. Mouse's sense of unease grew. Once more he called out to the darkness.

'Ralph, is that—'

Suddenly a hand shot forward and gripped him tightly about the throat.

'My, ain't we talking posh these days,' purred a voice like the voice of the darkness itself. 'So ain't ya going to say something nice to y'dear big brother then? After all, Mouse, it's been quite a while.'

CHAPTER FOURTEEN

At that moment Mouse was too shocked to put up any resistance. But when Vinnie grabbed his collar to drag him down the stairs, he began to squirm, and flail, and kick out.

'No, Vinnie!' he screamed. 'Don't want to go with you! Want to stay here!'

'But your little adventure's over, Mouse,' growled Vinnie. 'Now y're coming 'ome to y'proper family an' all y'friends. You'll *see* just 'ow much they missed ya.'

'No, Vinnie . . . please!'

The commotion echoed throughout the house—sounding like a battle, threatening to bring the entire staircase crashing down. Dangerously it creaked, sending falls of powdered stone trickling into the darkness. On the ground floor a door opened wide enough for an eye to peer out. Old Joe watched, his gaze fixed upon Vinnie's leather jacket.

'Nazis!' he hissed, his voice trembling with hatred and fear. For emblazoned across the back of the jacket was the Nazis' evil emblem—the *swastika*—picked out in silver studs that caught the little light there was and shone. And once again Joe was back in Warsaw with the rubble heaped up in the streets and the burnt-out trams, and the sinister midnight calls of the secret police.

'*Gestapo!*'

He breathed out the word as if it hurt, and his door closed and a key clicked firmly in the lock.

Outside, the night air was brittle with frost. Headlights flashed on. Harsh and blinding—like searchlights.

Seeing the dark Mercedes waiting for him, Mouse put up a last desperate struggle to be free. Vinnie could hardly hold him. He swore and with a final shove bundled Mouse into the back seat. Fear then crushed the boy. The cloying smell of leather upholstery mixed with expensive cologne caught in his throat making him breathe uneasily. In front of him, Pinner's dark shape rose broad behind the steering wheel. Without a word he leant back and landed Mouse a smarting blow to the face.

'That's for all the trouble you caused me, lad,' he said in a nasty monotone.

'You tell 'im, Mr Pinner,' grinned Vinnie,

slipping into the front passenger seat beside him. 'Little trouble-maker, ain't ya, Mouse?'

'Shut it,' growled Pinner, in his present mood both volatile and dangerous.

The limo moved away, picking up speed until it was churning up gravel in a rattling spray. And there, by the dark shrubbery, momentarily caught in the headlights, stood a serious, round-faced boy, his hands thrust deep into the pockets of his Barbour coat.

'Ralph,' murmured Mouse.

But it was Pinner who lifted a hand to acknowledge him. And it was to Pinner Ralph returned the wave. It was Ralph who had betrayed him.

The bare walls; the stained mattress; the crumpled, coarse blankets; the dismal view of dark roofs and crumbling chimney stacks. Mouse's old room was depressingly unchanged. Only this time, when he tried the door, it was locked against him. As soon as work in the shop was done his room became his cell.

At such times, when he was alone, was he free to think. About Annie and Clyde . . . and yes, even Ralph—the old Ralph. Did they remember him as much as he remembered them? They had become his past; he thought of them every day.

He grew increasingly more lonely. In the shop it was rare that anyone took notice of him. The Saturday boys thought him dull to the point of being stupid—besides, he was Vinnie's brother, which made them all the more guarded. Nobody trusted Vinnie.

During tea-breaks Mouse might not have existed, for he had nothing to add to the general chatter. His only stories concerned his brief time at Coldby and he doubted whether they would believe him. There'd be sniggers and nudges and then he'd be branded a liar as well as an idiot. In any case he had sworn secrecy on the matter and even now, despite all that had happened, his promise was binding.

After their breaks it was Mouse's job to wash up the mugs, then he was expected to wait upon Pinner. Pinner's coffee was kept in a locked cupboard. Filter coffee—not instant—two sweeteners and just a splash of milk. Instead of a mug he had a special cup and saucer; and he would grind his teeth and shout if it was not exactly right.

One Friday morning Mouse knocked on his door as usual, entering when bid.

Pinner glanced up from behind his desk and grunted. 'You 'ave to go round w'that hard done by face, lad?' he muttered. 'You'll scare my customers away with a face like that.'

Mouse didn't want to smile. He had nothing to smile about. Setting down Pinner's coffee he began to back away. As he did so something caught his eye. It was a model, as big as a table top, showing carefully contoured hills, with trees and roads and little scaled-down houses and cars.

Immediately the boy felt a sense of unease yet he didn't know why. Ignoring Pinner's presence he crossed over to examine the model more closely.

The detail was incredible. The little houses were either mock-Tudor or neo-Georgian, each with its own tiny green patch of garden. Yet Mouse's feeling of apprehension grew as he followed a road with his eyes until they came to a much larger building at the centre. He knew it at once but was shocked to see it there. It was Coldby Hall. Alongside it lay a sign: *Clubhouse and Hotel*. He also saw that a golf-course and access road devoured much of Jerusalem Wood, the remainder being relegated to *Woodland Feature*.

'So you know what it is then?' said Pinner slowly, without looking up.

'You can't—'

'Can't? You 'ave to move with the times, boy. Push an' shove. Push an' shove. Do it before someone else shoves you—that's my motto. And I ain't done too badly by it, neither. Jus' you think on, that old wreck o' a stately 'ome ain't always been there. It represented progress for its age—and that model is the way ahead for ours.'

'What about Joe?'

'The old geezer?' Pinner blew out contemptuously. ''E's 'ad 'is day, too and should stand aside for what's up and coming. I'm sure your brother Vinnie and 'is pal Jinks can convince 'im of the advantages in selling up. For one thing 'e'll be much safer in some old folks' 'ome.'

He made this sound a threat should Joe get in his way. But how would Joe survive in an old people's home, surrounded by strangers who knew nothing about him or the life that made him how he was? They would simply dismiss him as a crazy old man.

Back in the shop, Mouse went automatically about his work. He appeared no different to anyone who glanced his way, but underneath his mind was awash with thoughts. What might be done? What ought to be done? What could be done? His answer always came up the same. Nothing. Pinner's sort will always win. At the end of the day he was simply a powerful bully. Progress was an excuse he gave for getting his own way and making stacks of money in the process. He didn't care for anything or anyone. And to think Ralph believed he was interested in a few old beer bottles. It was so obvious now, he was merely stringing the boy along, while all the time looking beyond him at a far greater prize, that of the house and its land—

'Mouse.'

Someone softly spoke his name, waking him from his thoughts.

Raising his head he looked into Annie's dark, concerned eyes. His mouth fell open, but he was unable to speak or utter a single sound. His hands gestured vaguely and he went on stacking the empty shelves.

'I came . . . ' she said in a low hesitant voice. 'I came because I had to . . . because of Ralph and what he did . . . Listen, Mouse— please—he's so sorry, you know. You've seen how he gets—how he is . . . He has an idea one minute—good or bad—and the next he just does it. He's so brainy in some ways; other times he doesn't think about things at all . . . and now . . . now he's sorry . . . Really sorry . . . You have to believe me, Mouse. It's the truth.'

Mouse regarded her harshly. 'Well, I see you've bought his story hook, line, and sinker,' he said bitterly. 'I ought to have known you Pendreds would stick together. You always did.'

'Not always, Mouse . . . Oh yes, I suppose

we have, but that's not the reason Ralph didn't come here himself.'

'Oh, isn't it?' said Mouse sarcastically.

'No—Pinner would recognize him, that's all.'

She sighed.

'You're Ralph's only friend,' she said after a moment's silence. 'I mean, at school none of the other kids like him. Think he's full of himself and big ideas. And you've seen our house. Mum cleans offices at nights. Oh, she tries her best, but she doesn't finish until eleven o'clock; and we haven't a dad, so Ralph has always been in charge. Since I can remember he's played the pretend game. He wanted to pretend that we were rich, with all the money we'd ever need. When we discovered the bottles it got to be more than make believe. And you, you came along and wanted to pretend things of your own; and Ralph was happy to go along with it, so we were all happy. Until now.' She touched his arm. 'We miss you, Mouse. All of us. We want you to come back. It's different now.'

Mouse bowed his head. Two heavy tears dripped to the floor.

'Ah well . . . ' he shrugged, drawing the back of his hand across his nose and sniffing hard. A while later, when composed, he said, 'I suppose you know Pinner's after the hall?

He's told my brother Vinnie and his mate Jinks to scare Joe into selling it.'

She nodded. 'Poor Joe's already half frightened to death. They roar around the hall at midnight on their motor bikes, and throw stones at his windows. Really childish things—but Joe's convinced they're the gas . . . gas . . .'

'*Gestapo*,' corrected Mouse. 'They were the German secret police in the Second World War. Joe told me about them.'

'So you see,' said the girl, 'we need you. You must come back and help—for Joe's sake.'

'How can I—'

Suddenly Annie's eyes widened. Pinner was coming. Hastily she pressed a ball of paper into Mouse's hand, turned and hurried from the shop.

Mouse just managed to conceal the paper up his sleeve before he felt Pinner breathing down his neck. He stared after Annie through the plate glass window. Waiting for her across the road was Ralph. For a moment the eyes of the two boys made contact. Uncertainly Ralph raised his hand and waved.

'Ain't you done yet?'

Pinner's demanding tone forced Mouse to turn away. When next he looked, both Annie and Ralph had gone.

CHAPTER FIFTEEN

Mouse didn't examine the piece of paper Annie had given him, at least not straight away. He enjoyed prolonging the suspense—it was like waiting to unwrap a special parcel. Later, hidden from prying eyes, he reached into his sleeve and retrieved the crumpled ball, spreading it flat before him. He found it was a letter in Ralph's small spiky handwriting. Devouring each word at a time, this is what he read:

Dear Mouse,
I don't blame you if you hate me—really hate me I mean. It was a pretty mean and cowardly trick. But believe me when I say I hate myself far worse than you ever will. Please—please—please say you'll forget about it and start again. If you do I'll try to put things right at once. Tonight we'll be waiting for you across the road in the Land Rover. We'll be there from seven to eight o'clock. I needn't tell you

that the Land Rover shouldn't be on the road at all (no tax, insurance, at least two bald tyres, etc.) and I certainly shouldn't be behind the wheel. So try to make it as early as possible in case we draw attention to ourselves.

Best regards,

Your friend,

Ralph.

p.s. Remember Mouse, seven to eight o'clock. It'll be great seeing you again.

And in a more rounded, childish hand:

p.p.s. It's me, Clyde. Hello, Mouse. I hope you do come back and live with us again.

Mouse hugged the letter to himself and began to think. He knew his best chance to escape was now while the main doors were open for business. But then what? Vinnie and Jinks were sure to come looking for him—and bound to catch him so close to the shop if he hung around waiting for Ralph. On the other hand, later on when the time was right, he would be securely locked in his room.

'And if I don't turn up,' Mouse whispered to himself, 'Ralph'll think it's because I don't want to.'

The thought made him unbelievably miserable.

Crushing the paper in his hand, he pushed it back up his sleeve, hurrying into the shop before he was missed.

It may have been his imagination, of course, but now, whenever he looked up, the security cameras seemed to be pointing in his direction; or Pinner's shadowy form was looming over him in the one-way mirror that linked the back rooms to the shop; or Vinnie was chasing him to help unload a van or bring something down from the stockroom.

Yet while his every movement might be observed, his thoughts remained his own. Slowly Mouse's plan took shape in his head.

When next he was sent upstairs to fetch something from the stockroom, he took the opportunity to try out his idea. Turning off the stairwell he made his way along the dingy corridor to his room. Working as quickly as he could he took a little stuffing from his mattress and rolled it between his thumb and first finger until it was a hard ball about the size of a bean.

This being done, he turned his attention to the bolt. The sliding part was screwed to the door, and the little brass hoop, which housed it when thrown across, was secured to the door-frame. Into that hoop Mouse now worked the tiny wad of stuffing.

At first he was clumsy in his haste—all

thumbs—expecting at any moment Pinner or Vinnie to rise up behind him, demanding to know what he was doing. However, after the first few minutes, his heart ceased to beat quite so fast, and calmly he tested his handiwork . . . It couldn't have been better. Nervously he allowed himself a smile. Of course, he realized his plan depended on an element of luck, too. It would totally collapse should Vinnie notice that the bolt didn't fit properly when it came to locking - up time that evening; and until that moment Mouse had no way of knowing for sure if his plan would succeed or fail.

'Mouse! Mouse!' suddenly Vinnie's harsh voice was summoning him from below.

The afternoon dragged interminably. The very act of waiting made Mouse weary. Worn down by suspense his movements became sluggish, while any sudden noise made him start violently.

'Wass up wi' you?' asked Vinnie with his customary bluntness. 'Like a cat on a 'ot tin roof t'day.'

'S-sorry, Vin,' Mouse mumbled.

At half-past five the till women cashed up and stood chatting and yawning. Pinner put out the main lights. The women crowded off home, their coats buttoned up to conceal their milk-maid outfits which none of them liked.

'G'night, Mr Pinner.'

' 'Night,' replied Pinner gruffly, standing by the door ready to lock up and switch on the security system.

'Still on f'tonight, Mr Pinner?' Vinnie sidled up and asked.

Pinner gave a single nod, then indicated *quiet* because Mouse was within earshot.

Vinnie bought fish and chips for himself and Mouse and they sat down at an 'antique' table to eat them. Vinnie was bright-eyed and excited, as he always was before doing one of Pinner's special jobs.

'You'll 'ave to be in ya room early t'night,' he told Mouse. 'I suppose you'll be whinging on at me to borrow m'telly again.'

'No. It's all right,' replied Mouse quietly. 'Don't want it. Honest.'

Vinnie regarded him suspiciously. 'Why you keep looking at the clock?' he asked.

Mouse reacted with genuine surprise. 'I don't, Vin. Do I?'

Vinnie grunted. 'Waste o' time you looking in any case,' he said. 'Not like you got somewhere t'go.'

'No, Vin.'

Angrily Vinnie snatched up the greasy chip papers and beat them into a ball. 'Waste o' money that were. You 'ardly touched any o' it.'

'Soss, Vin. Just not hungry.'

'You're not turning ill on me? Couldn't stand that.' He got to his feet. 'Anyway, up t'your room. Ain't got all night to go nursemaiding it round.'

Mouse was pale with excitement as they climbed the stairs, his breathing so shallow he gasped for air. Within the next five minutes he would know the outcome of his plan. What if Vinnie noticed? What then? He closed his mind to the possibility, unable to think beyond the present.

Just then Vinnie shot a glance back at him, catching him unaware. 'You sure y'ain't feeling bad?' he said.

'I'm fine. Tired that's all.'

'Just as well,' grinned Vinnie, 'as ya in for an early night.'

He lifted his hand to switch on the light, allowing Mouse a sly glimpse of his wristwatch. Already it was five past seven.

'In you go,' ordered Vinnie.

Mouse stepped into his room. The door closed. He remained standing, blood pounding in his ears. The bolt rattled. Then, instead of its customary click, he heard a soft thud as the bolt met the little wad of stuffing. To his own ears the difference was painfully clear.

He stood frozen, his face turned to the door. Was Vinnie aware that something was wrong? If not, why hadn't he moved away? The blood beat louder as if he were about to faint. Then suddenly he heard Vinnie's footsteps clumping down the corridor, and letting out a long sigh fell forwards across the mattress, bouncing up the moment he struck it. There wasn't a second to waste. Resting his hand on the door handle he turned it and gave a gentle shove.

It was locked.

Mouse was neither surprised nor dismayed at this point. He had allowed just enough space in the metal hoop to make it appear as if the bolt had properly slid home. The real trick lay in shaking the door to gradually ease the bolt free. In previous practices he had managed to do this in no more than thirty seconds.

Quickly the minutes mounted and an element of despair crept into the boy's actions. He kicked the door and swore. The door rattled and rattled but refused to budge. He thought of his friends waiting for him and began hurling himself at the door, shouting 'Ralph! Annie!' not caring if he got hurt.

However, when next he turned the handle, the door obediently swung open for him. After trying for what seemed hours, Mouse stared at it in astonishment. But not for long. Stepping into the unlit corridor he turned off his light, watching as the red filament cooled and merged into the dark.

Without light it was impossible to go more than three steps before stumbling over an empty tea-chest or packing case. Spreading his arms, Mouse found his fingertips could just touch either wall. Then, keeping his sight fixed to the crack of light edging the distant door on to the main staircase, he shuffled his way forwards. He tried to make as little noise as possible and his ears strained to catch any other sounds that might pin-point the whereabouts of Vinnie and Pinner. The prospect of meeting either one on the stairs was too terrible to contemplate.

Carefully he opened the door. No one was there, so he slipped out on to the landing, where each of his steps was an agent for Pinner, creaking out its tell-tale warning as the boy shifted his weight on to it. He climbed upwards a step at a time, until he reached the grimy window that opened on to the fire-escape.

Suddenly he stopped dead, his arms stretched out and swaying for balance like a man on a tightrope, frozen by the sound of Pinner's voice.

'Come on, Vinnie, get your tail into motion,' he snarled. 'What we waiting for now? I want this visit to that stubborn old buzzard at Coldby over and done with. I get the feelin' the old boy might do business t'night.'

'Sorry, Mr Pinner,' came Vinnie's diffident reply. He was almost directly underneath the spot where Mouse now stood. 'Ain't me. Jinks ain't back yet. 'E nipped out a while ago f'some ciggies.'

Pinner mumbled something that Mouse did not catch—mainly because he was concentrating so hard on the window. Bit by bit he raised the sash, and like a thief slipped through the opening into the night. The fire-escape rang metallically as he hurried down it to the street below. Beneath a lamp-post he saw the familiar battered Land Rover. He saw pale faces inside it. All at once they turned to him. He saw smiles. He reached the bottom of the fire-escape, needing only to cross the street to be with them.

Then it all went wrong. The three faces stopped smiling and hands urgently waved at him to go back. Just in time he spotted Jinks swaggering up the street, whistling tunelessly and jangling his keys. Unable to retreat up the fire-escape without being seen, Mouse slipped through the double gates into the yard where Pinner parked his Mercedes. But now he heard Pinner and Vinnie coming out from the building. Desperate for somewhere to hide, he opened the car's boot and clambered in, holding down the lid just wide enough to see out.

'Come on, Jinks!' roared Pinner. 'Ain't no 'oliday I'm paying you for.'

The car rolled slightly as Pinner climbed in. Its engine started and the two motor bikes roared; the car followed them from the yard with Mouse, its unwilling passenger, holding on as best he could.

Luckily the Pendreds had seen what had happened. Peering back down the road, Mouse saw the Land Rover splutter into life, emerging from a cloud of its own exhaust fumes to give chase. Along the busy thoroughfares he was able to track its progress by its distinctive headlights (being closer and higher than those of other vehicles); while the throaty roar of its engine was equally as unmistakable. But for all that, it was no match for the Mercedes which, beneath Pinner's hands, slipped in and out of the traffic, as if he were king of the road. Other cars frequently squeezed between them and twice Mouse feared that Ralph had lost him. But somehow the Land Rover always managed to come back.

At the edge of town traffic thickened. Steadily the Land Rover nosed its way through, until once more positioned right behind the Mercedes. Now all Mouse needed was an opportune moment. This presented itself at a busy junction, where the traffic flow came to a halt in a bumper-to-bumper queue.

Mouse knew he was taking a risk, but who could say if he would have the chance again. Throwing wide the boot lid he jumped out and ran. He ran to the back of the Land Rover and hurled himself in.

'Get your foot down, Ralph,' he shouted, spreading himself flat across the floor.

'But—'

'Just do it!'

Mouse felt the Land Rover lurch to overtake the Mercedes, narrowly missing Pinner who had stepped out to investigate. Horns blared angrily as the Land Rover drove straight into the path of oncoming traffic. Annie sharply drew her breath, tyres screamed and, with the engine straining as it picked up revs, they skidded around the junction towards Coldby.

CHAPTER SIXTEEN

Suddenly everyone burst out laughing, breaking the awful tension of the moment; and all at once they began talking without anyone listening—which didn't matter, since most talk consisted of garbled nonsense; and hands reached back to touch Mouse as if they couldn't believe it was him; and all he could find to say was, 'I'm all right . . . I'm fine . . . I'm okay . . . '

Then, glancing up at the driving mirror, Ralph saw the headlights of two motor cycles weave in and out of the traffic, gaining on them even as he watched. They had forgotten Jinks and Vinnie. Soon Jinks's machine lay on their tail, its headlight reflecting from the mirror in sharp dazzling beams; while Vinnie drew up alongside. He wore a helmet and goggles; and the wind, catching his face, pulled back his cheeks into a hard, uncompromising frown.

No sooner had he appeared than a terrific

bang was heard on the driver's side. Clyde squealed. First thoughts were that the Land Rover and motor bike had collided. But then Vinnie struck out a second time with his boot. He did so repeatedly; and they saw him mouthing ugly curses. Oncoming vehicles sounded their horns to warn the lunatic motor cyclist riding the white lines of the road. Yet if this was a game of nerves, it wasn't Vinnie's nerve that broke first: he let others brake and swerve.

'He looks really mad,' said Annie peering at him from behind Ralph. 'Can't we go any faster?'

'We're thrashing the old crate as it is,' said Ralph. 'I'll try to shake them off at the Roughlands.'

'*Roughlands*?' said Mouse, squeezing himself between the two seats. 'What are they?'

'It's the old heath land leading to Jerusalem Wood,' explained Ralph, half turning his head towards him. 'It's pretty bumpy, but at least there's no stopping to open gates,' and he added, 'I'll try to make up on time so we can give Joe plenty of warning.'

'Poor old Joe,' said Mouse. 'All he ever wanted was the quiet life. Wh~~~ ~ understand is, why doesn't he ~~~~ police?'

'You know Joe,' replied Annie. 'He doesn't trust anyone in uniform. He thinks it makes them a soldier.'

'Besides,' added Ralph somewhat guiltily, 'he's worried they'll discover his illegal vodka still.'

'Even so,' said Mouse, 'the cops'll have to be called in at some stage or matters'll get right out of hand. Someone might end up getting hurt.'

They drove on another three miles with the bikes elegantly and persistently buzzing them like a pair of angry hornets.

Suddenly a signpost appeared and Ralph shouted, 'Hang on!'

With no indication he skidded across the main road into a deserted country lane. His foot barely touched the brakes and all four tyres squealed fit to burst. But it worked. They had fooled Vinnie and Jinks who hammered past the turning and were forced to slow and wheel about. All in all Ralph's action had won a few precious seconds. When Mouse next looked over his shoulder, he saw headlights sweep around the corner and, like arms, reach out after them.

'Hold tight again!' cried Ralph.

Yanking the wheel hard he turned off the lane. The others thought he had gone mad ˙nd driven over a cliff. They seemed to hang endlessly in the air. Annie and Clyde tipped forward with a shriek and would have struck the windscreen had their safety belts not restrained them. Mouse, who had nothing to hold him back, dug his nails into the seats, tense against the inevitable crash. But the Land Rover gradually caught the slope of the land and bumped everyone back into their places again. The wildly swaying headlights revealed snatches of broken ground, dotted here and there by small dark trees.

Off the road the journey rapidly deteriorated into an endless battery of jolts and lurches. Inside the cab everything loose or not secured rattled and clanked, as if the vehicle were disintegrating around their ears.

The one consolation for its four passengers lay in the knowledge that it was far worse for Vinnie and Jinks. Despite the latest gadgetry and ability to eat up countless miles of road, their machines were not trail bikes—they were the wrong shape for one thing, and their tyres were too narrow with too shallow a tread. Mouse also derived extra malicious pleasure imagining every inch of highly-polished chrome on his brother's motor bike slowly becoming encrusted with mud. Their powerful engines roared uselessly, the power all lost to skids and greasily spinning wheels.

Probably Ralph would have out-run them

completely, had the Land Rover not chosen that moment to wheelspin itself to a standstill in a patch of soft ground. It strained, each time almost on the point of coming free, yet each time slipping back into the mire again.

'We're stuck fast!' Ralph said slapping the wheel in frustration.

Mouse was worried. 'We can't just sit here,' he said. 'Better to get out and make a run for it while we still can.'

'No,' said Ralph firmly. 'You three climb down. Let's see if you can't push us out of this one.'

As Annie, Clyde, and Mouse got down from the cab, they saw the two motor bikes in the distance.

'Turn off your lights, Ralph,' shouted Mouse. 'It might keep them off our backs for a while.'

'Not if they're following our tyre tracks,' muttered Clyde gloomily.

Nevertheless Ralph obliged and in darkness they pushed for all they were worth, the drone of the approaching motor bikes adding extra urgency to their efforts.

'It's not budging!' gasped Clyde falling wearily against the tail-gate.

'Try rocking it,' said Annie. 'Push, then let it roll back and push again.'

They tried it her way. This time the Land

Rover gained momentum, slowed, appeared as though it might stop and roll back, but then continued, pulling itself inch by inch free of the trench it had settled into.

They ran to climb in. A backwards glance revealed to Mouse how close the leading biker now was. From the designs on his crash helmet he knew it to be Jinks.

'Quickly, Mouse—get in!' implored Ralph. He began accelerating away before Mouse was properly aboard.

Slipping and sliding, Jinks managed to draw up alongside. They saw how he fought to restrain his back wheel, which was constantly trying to swing out and spin the whole machine around. He used his foot—heel down in the mud—as a rudder to steer by and to gain extra stability. He even looked up and grinned at the children, seeking their admiration for his skills.

'Jinks used to do speedway,' said Mouse. 'He's good at this sort of thing.'

There was a grim little smile on Ralph's face as he said, 'Let's see what he can make of this.'

Deliberately he pulled the Land Rover to the right.

Clyde and Annie cried out at the same time.

'You'll run him over!'

'Look out!'

Ralph, however, seemed to know what he was doing. He caught the bike a glancing blow. It hardly made a sound, but its effect was remarkable. Jinks completely lost control as his bike was deflected at gathering speed down the steep slope of a pit. The brake light flashed red, but too late. Hitting a lip of stone Jinks was catapulted from his saddle. Riderless the bike reared like a wild horse, its headlight pointing skywards; then, in a series of crazy somersaults, it tumbled away into a dark tangle of gorse and brambles that lay much further below.

'Hooray!' shouted Clyde excitedly.

Annie glanced behind. 'But there's still Mouse's brother,' she said.

'And he's no walk-over like Jinks,' said Mouse, who knew how his brother's cold stealth worked. But at least the distance between them continued to grow.

Soon Jerusalem Wood appeared through the cracked windscreen. By skirting its boundary, Ralph arrived on familiar territory once more, and was able to put his foot down. Coming over the ridge they saw the hall, pale and faintly luminous, in the hollow below.

'Can you see Pinner's car?' asked Mouse, frantically looking himself.

No—nobody could.

Ralph braked, letting everyone spill out.

'Joe! Joe!'

They ran up the steps and beat upon his door. Clyde shouted through the letter box.

'Joe, open up. . . Joe!'

They persisted until the door was violently flung open and there stood the old man in his grubby dressing gown. His eyes were red and his hair uncombed. He glared at them as if at unwelcome strangers.

'Listen, Joe,' pleaded Ralph. 'We have to get you out of here. For your own good. There's going to be more rough stuff tonight.'

Joe waved his hand, irritated and dismissing. 'Da damn Nazis,' he croaked. 'Let them com'. I damn ready thiz time. You tell them com'. Tell them Joseph Dabrowski, he ready, and never vill he run avay from them again.'

'Listen, Joe—'

'I once damn fine *polski* officer. Thiz my home. They tak' everything from me in Poland. Thiz time I make stand. I fight.'

He reached into the shadows and lifted something heavy.

'Joe—what are you doing with a gun?' gasped Annie. 'Oh, Joe, please, don't be silly—this will all end in big trouble—'

'Ya, big trouble coming—for *them*.'

The old man stood prepared, something of the old soldier shining down the years. He held the shotgun across his chest, alert and ready to use it.

Ralph started pushing Annie away saying, 'Quickly—take Clyde. Get down to the village. Dial 999. Get the police. Tell 'em it's an emergency.'

'I want to see Joe shoot someone,' howled Clyde as Annie took his arm and dragged him away.

Once they were clear, the two boys begged and reasoned with Joe to see sense; Ralph grew so desperate he even attempted to snatch the weapon from his hands. But the old man had the iron of his resolve. He pushed the boys aside babbling a string of Polish curses at them. Then his whole body stiffened as he heard the distant sound of a motor bike.

'Vinnie,' uttered Mouse.

The motor bike was approaching at speed, and all eyes fixed upon a belt of overgrown rhododendrons from behind which it would eventually appear. The old man gripped his shotgun, and Mouse and Ralph heard it click ominously. '*Nazywam sie Joseph Dabrowski*,' he repeated over and over like a prayer.

Then Vinnie was there, racing clear to the other side of the hall before Joe had time to lift the gun to his shoulder. Now he stood with it raised and ready for firing, his bloodshot eye squinting down the wavering barrel.

It was too much to hope that Vinnie had seen the old man with the gun and fled. Sure enough, shortly afterwards he reappeared, slowing to stop. Mouse saw a finger curl around the trigger and, as much as he hated his brother, had no desire to see him dead or badly injured. He leapt at Joe.

Bang!

The shot veered uselessly into the trees.

Ears ringing and blinded by the brilliant flash, Mouse lost his footing and rolled down the steps. Ralph rushed to his aid. A cartridge clattered from the gun.

'Ralph! Don't let him shoot Vinnie,' shouted Mouse as he lay on the ground.

But Ralph was too far away to prevent him. Grimly taking aim, Joe pulled the trigger a second time; no sooner did the shot ring out than there followed the terrible sound of metal exploding. Bike and rider went flying through the air, the bike's rear wheel reduced to a tangled mass of twisted chrome and shredded rubber.

'Vinnie!' screamed Mouse.

Vinnie lay on his back, seemingly broken and lifeless.

Mouse went scrambling across to his side.

'Oh, Vin,' he sobbed.

'You stinking little—'

Quick as a whip, Vinnie's gauntleted hand

shot out seizing Mouse's ankle. Mouse gasped in surprise, then his other foot came down hard on Vinnie's wrist and, when Vinnie jerked his hand away, Mouse went flying back to the hall.

On the steps, Joe was no less agitated than before, hurling out a stream of abuse in his native tongue—not at Vinnie this time but at something further down the drive. He lifted the reloaded gun and let fly a third shot. Mouse turned his head in time to see Pinner's windscreen shatter into a thousand splinters, radiating from a single jagged hole. As he watched, Pinner himself appeared, pale and shaken, throwing himself down in a ditch for cover.

The abandoned Mercedes, with its purring engine, bright lights, and wide open door, made a sitting target, even for someone with failing eyesight. A fourth shot demolished the radiator, a fifth and sixth peppered the bonnet, and a seventh put out a headlight.

Joe chuckled, taking pleasure from his sport; in contrast a savage roar arose in the darkness every time the vehicle was struck.

'You're a madman,' bellowed Pinner. 'I'll see you put away for this! Put away for ever!'

Fire was flickering from the dashboard when Joe finally ran out of ammunition. Seeing their chance, Mouse and Ralph grabbed his arms and bundled him into the hallway, bolting the door behind them. Then Joe's strength gave out and he became a frail old man again. The hot gun dropped from his hands, clattering across the tiles.

'Now you've set the cat among the pigeons,' whispered Ralph.

'They should leave me be,' replied Joe, still faintly defiant.

A fist pounding on the door silenced them.

'You know what you've done, you . . . you . . . madman?' spluttered Pinner from the other side. 'You've written off my Merc. *Look* at it! Forty-five grand's worth o' German technology goin' up in smoke because of you . . . you . . . you . . . worthless old joker.' And with more menace he said, 'You wait till I get me 'ands on you. You jus' wait!'

'And what about m'bike?' came Vinnie's distant wail. 'I ain't even insured.'

'Shud up!' bellowed Pinner unsympathetically. 'Go fetch a log or some'in'. I pay you to break into places—so get me through this door!'

Their footsteps died away.

'Come on,' said Mouse. 'Upstairs.'

'Why?' asked Ralph.

'You'll see.'

With no little effort they pushed and cajoled Joe to the top of the building.

'Vhy all theze damn bottles in my house?' he asked, glancing around the darkened room into which he was finally led. There was no time for explanations. Throwing wide the window Mouse peered out at the scene below, his view well illuminated by the fiery car. He saw Vinnie nervously running back and forth across the gravel, pursued by Pinner endlessly demanding, 'Do some'in'!' In the flickering orange light their shadows were as spindly as stick insects.

Then, acting out of sheer desperation, Vinnie reached down, snatched up a large stone and hurled it through the nearest window. The sound of shattering glass reached every empty room in the hall.

'They'll easily get through a window,' said Ralph, standing behind Mouse and gazing over his shoulder.

'Not if I can stop them,' grinned Mouse and he held up an old beer bottle.

'No, Mouse!' cried Ralph in dismay. 'That one's worth at least—' Mouse stared hard at him and Ralph quickly relented. 'Okay, you're right,' he said. Giving a resigned shrug he picked up a bottle, too.

Mouse, meanwhile, had taken up his position, leaning out from the window as far as he dared. He spent time carefully taking aim, tracing his intended target as it moved.

Only when he was sure of hitting the mark did he release the bottle, casually letting it slip free of his grasp.

Crack!

It was a perfect shot, striking Vinnie on the top of his head (just as well he was wearing a crash helmet). Taken by surprise, Vinnie reeled backwards until his legs twisted about each other and collapsed beneath him. Mouse grinned broadly. If he never achieved anything more, his life would have been worthwhile for that one glorious moment.

'Well done,' laughed Ralph, patting him on the back. 'Now let's see what I can do.'

He threw down his bottle and saw it explode into fragments at Pinner's feet. The next minute Joe was shoving them aside, his arms bursting with beer bottles. Inelegantly, he unloaded the whole lot straight out of the window—the noise they made upon striking the ground made the boys wince.

Joe beamed at them, looking mighty pleased with himself. 'Ha!' he cackled. 'Theze damn fine *Molotov cocktailz*. Together ve defend *Warszawa*, no? Ve fight on and make all Poland free!'

'For Poland and freedom!' yelled Ralph, and Mouse gave a rebel yell.

Unceasingly the bottles rained down on Pinner and Vinnie who ran wildly before them, bumbling into each other as they tried to escape. In no time broken glass lay scattered everywhere, sparkling like frost in the light of the fire.

'All right, enough is enough,' conceded Pinner, crouching on his knees and cradling his head for protection. But victory was assured in any case. From high up in the house its three defenders saw a flashing blue light.

'It's the police!' cried Ralph and a short while later they heard a siren.

'We've won . . . we've won!' Ralph grabbed Joe's hands and spun him round and round like the bag of bones he was. 'We've beaten old Pinner—we've won!'

He turned to Mouse and saw him standing quietly by the window.

'Mouse . . . What is it?'

At first Mouse didn't answer; he was too absorbed in watching the car as it steadily burnt, throwing up a dense oily cloud of smoke. When he did speak his voice sounded oddly distant.

'It's all come back to me, Ralph,' he said. 'I remember . . . the crash with Mum and Dad . . . and the moment before the crash . . . and being small . . . and . . . I remember everything again . . . Everything.'

CHAPTER SEVENTEEN

Just before midday some weeks later Detective
Inspector Richardson drove his unmarked car
up the track to Coldby Hall. The pale sun was
melting the frost and he drove at a leisurely
rate, his eyes forever darting upwards at the
sky. The detective inspector was an
ornithologist—a bird-watcher—who kept his
spare pair of binoculars on the back seat for
lax moments such as these. His excuse to
himself was that it kept his senses keen—made
him sharper at observing. Why, some of these
new bobbies could walk straight through a
bank robbery and not see a blind thing.

Noticing a hovering dot, he suddenly pulled
over to the side and wound the window down.
Through the binoculars the detective
inspector watched it in close detail for what it
really was—a beautiful young sparrowhawk,
perhaps a migrant from Scandinavia, passing
its winter above the unspoilt grounds of

Coldby Hall.

He continued to watch until the hawk swooped low and was lost from sight. Reluctantly, he placed the binoculars on the seat beside him, his hand brushing yesterday's newspaper. The local press was milking the latest crime for all it was worth. *Business Man Operated Antiques Crime Ring*, blazed the headline, reminding the detective inspector of the real purpose behind his visit, so he pushed the car into gear and drove on.

He still hadn't fathomed out this case. Not entirely. On the face of it, it revolved around a group of kids—and that old Pole, of course. He sighed, remembering the trouble the old man had caused, locking himself in his room if he so much as glimpsed a police uniform (the reason why the detective inspector himself was required to pay this otherwise routine call). They had been as free as anything with damning information concerning Pinner and his gang yet, on other matters, they remained resolutely silent. Still, Pinner was the big fish. They had caught him with a warehouse of stolen antiques and other incriminating evidence. Those two roughnecks, his accomplices, were due for long prison stretches, too. Most judges are old men who take a dim view of anyone terrorizing other old men.

The detective inspector frowned as he considered the case's unresolved elements. By far the biggest mystery was the whereabouts of Vinnie's younger brother—Samuel Robert—or *Mouse* as he was nicknamed. He had disappeared off the face of the earth. Where do people go when they disappear like that? Wherever it was, Mouse had gone there too, slipping away the minute the police showed at the scene. And what a scene it was. More like the aftermath of a riot, with the burning car and all that broken glass. And that was another thing. Where did so much glass come from? Probably the kid—Mouse— was worried about being dragged down with Vinnie, so had taken himself off. But he needn't have worried. For him there were no charges to answer.

The inspector stopped his car and got out. He walked past a boarded-up window and knocked at the hall's door, noting with pleasure as he did so a house-martins' colony tucked beneath its eaves.

He knocked again when no one came, calling, 'Police. Anyone home?'

Of course, he knew full well there was, and kept knocking until the door opened just enough for a suspicious eye to glare out.

'Police,' he said again with great patience.

'*Policja?*' said the voice from inside. 'Vhat

doez police vant vith peazeful old man? Show me identification.'

The inspector fished his I.D. from his pocket and held it before the old man's face. Then the door opened to let him in.

'A fine old house this,' said the inspector, making conversation as he followed Joe into a room that smelt of plaster and paraffin.

Joe reacted as if to a criticism. 'Over three hundred year et stood here. Et vill stand three hundred more.'

'Don't mind me asking, sir,' continued the police officer, 'but don't you get a little lonely out here all by yourself?'

'I no alone,' snapped Joe.

'Oh?'

'I have cat, Napoleon.'

'I see, sir.' The inspector cleared his throat, saying in a more formal way, 'I just called in to say we won't be pressing charges concerning your unlicensed firearm. But we do intend to confiscate the weapon. Do you understand?'

Joe shrugged uncaringly. 'Next time I fight vith bare handz.'

'Hopefully, sir, there will be no next time, although I agree you were provoked by those hooligans.' He sighed heavily. 'If only you contacted us—the police—in the first place, an awful lot of unpleasantness could have been avoided. In the future, Mr Dabrowski, try giving us a ring rather than taking the law into your own hands.'

'You say there not be no next time,' cried Joe accusingly. '*You* keep my damn gun.'

'Er, indeed, sir.' The detective inspector turned to leave, then turned back. 'I suppose you've seen no trace of the missing boy—the one known as Mouse, who was here on the night?'

'*Nie!*' said Joe crossly. 'Vhy should I? Vild children vith no home ov their own. I damn good to them. They treat my houze az damn hotel. Com' and go az they pleaze. Now they go and leave me be—az I damn like et.'

The detective inspector saw he'd make no further progress with Joe. 'Ah well, Mr Dabrowski,' he said. 'I'll not intrude on your privacy any longer. Thanks for your help, I'll see myself out.'

'Ya,' snapped Joe rudely. 'Goodbye, Mr Polizeman.'

He didn't rise to see his visitor to the door, remaining seated in his chair, thoughtfully stroking Napoleon. But hearing the detective's car pull away he looked up and softly called, 'You com' out now, da *policjant* haz gone 'vay, hiz handz empty.'

Mouse appeared. He was grinning. He slipped from behind the door leading to the little kitchen and stood beside Joe.

'Thanks, Joe,' he said.

Joe squeezed his hand. 'You get me damn shot, boy,' he said, pretending to be angry. 'I no tell truth to da *policja*. Other old men have eazy life. Not Joseph Dabrowski.' He wheezed with laughter.

Mouse nodded, understanding full well the risk Joe had taken on his behalf. Without parents or relatives he would have been placed in care. But Joe genuinely wanted him to stay, and when the vodka was in him he would talk carelessly about some day leaving the hall to Mouse. (Although during his periodic bad moods he was just as quick to retract the idea, so who knew what the future held?)

At Joe's insistence, Mouse began to record all his earliest memories. Soon he had filled three old exercise books. At first the boy didn't understand the point, but then he discovered that a memory often had the power to trigger another. For instance, by remembering his father's oily fingers he also recalled that he worked in a garage; and from recollecting his mother's strong dislike of coffee, he remembered a picnic in a field on a hot sunny afternoon. Silly little throw-away things perhaps, but nevertheless important, too. Mouse even managed to recall happier times with Vinnie.

Mouse's books were eventually kept on the mantelpiece and Joe was in the habit of patting them and saying, 'Now, boy, vhatever happenz your past cannot go mizzing a second time.'

From keeping the exercise books sprang the idea that Joe would tutor Mouse, so he didn't lack an education as he grew up. The old man possessed an excellent brain for mathematics and the sciences, but his English left something to be desired ('you done a lot good' being a typical Joseph Dabrowski comment at the bottom of a page). As for history... Joe knew nothing of 1066, the Magna Carta, and the comings and goings of Tudor monarchs and Victorian prime ministers. History to him was the Hanseatic merchants, the Teutonic knights, Cosimir the Great, and Copernicus the star gazer.

Mouse spent so long in Joe's company that, unwittingly, he acquired a smattering of Polish, too. One day he said to Ralph, '*Dziekuje*' for thank you, and couldn't understand why the Pendreds gave him such an odd look and burst out giggling.

But then the Pendreds were always giggling.

Mouse saw them most evenings and every day at the weekends. When Christmas arrived Ralph blew most of the money saved from the Big Daddy on a spectacular party, driving up to the hall on Christmas Eve with the Land Rover bursting with presents and a Christmas tree so huge it only just squeezed through the door.

With the fire blazing and candles flickering, and with great swags of silver tinsel threatening to break and fall down on their heads at any moment, they sat eating, drinking, laughing, pulling crackers and singing carols.

Much later Joe stood up. He swayed on his feet and his paper hat was askew; and generally he was worse for wear on home-made vodka. (Nobody had seen the need to mention his <u>still</u> to the police.) After some sentimental thanks for a new silk dressing gown he proposed a toast.

Raising his jam jar he said, 'To our very good prezent and to our much better damn future. Good health! *Na zdrowie!*'

'*Na zdrowie!*' returned all four voices.

Lions

BERLIE DOHERTY
Street Child

Jim crept forward, invisible in the deep shadows, and stood, hardly breathing just inside the gate.

Jim Jarvis is a runaway. When his mother dies, Jim is all alone in the workhouse and is desperate to escape. But London in the 1860s is a dangerous and lonely place for a small boy and life is a constant battle for survival. Just when Jim finds some friends, he is snatched away and made to work for the remorselessly cruel Grimy Nick, constantly guarded by his vicious dog, Snipe.

Jim's gripping adventure is based on the true story of the orphan whose plight inspired Doctor Barnardo to set up his famous children's refuge.

Lions

NINA MILTON
Sweet 'n' Sour

Low felt breathless and tight inside. When he looked down, he found he'd folded the letter from England so many times, it was now a damp and grubby square no bigger than a postage stamp.

Low Hee's been living happily with his grandmother in Malaysia since he was born, so he's pretty annoyed when his father returns after seven years to take him to live in England. Life above the take-away restaurant is bleak - he can't speak any English or understand school *and* he's got a little sister no one has told him about.

But Low's life changes dramatically when he has an accident and changes places with Liang, the mysterious boy he has seen from his window...